*"Three months of days whose clarity is both perverse
and frightening, held without photographs or any
other telling semblance to prove I existed,
and that I survived...."*

In a debut novel of startling lyrical power, author Donald Rawley
re-creates the long, hot Southwestern summer of 1968 through the
eyes of ten-year-old Lindsay Paul ("L.P.") Fowler—a hard, pretty,
and effeminate only child in a wealthy Arizona family. Abandoned
without warning by his self-involved mother and cruel, dictatorial
grandmother, L.P. is sent off to spend a magical summer with Betty,
his grandmother's maid, in black South Phoenix. A former jazz
singer at war with inner demons of her own, Betty is the only adult
in L.P.'s small universe with room in her heart for the troubled
boy—offering him a friendship born of shared pain. And in a
remarkable season of fever dreams, betrayals, loss, and rude sexual
awakenings, L.P. will learn much about the fragile masks grown-ups
hide behind and the weapons they use to wound, setting him free
for flight, like the unseen night birds, singing in the dark.

"Rawley's style is sumptuous and baroque...
He has an uncanny knack for making the bizarre beautiful
and for capturing the pathos and peculiar dignity of characters
who wouldn't ordinarily command respect."
—*The Observer*

Other Avon Books by
Donald Rawley

SLOW DANCE ON THE FAULT LINE

Coming Soon

TINA IN THE BACK SEAT

THE NIGHT BIRD CANTATA

DONALD RAWLEY

AN AVON BOOK

This is a work of fiction. Names, characters, places, and incidents either are the product of the author's imagination or are used fictitiously. Any resemblance to actual events, locales, organizations, or persons, living or dead, is entirely coincidental and beyond the intent of either the author or the publisher.

AVON BOOKS, INC.
1350 Avenue of the Americas
New York, New York 10019

Copyright © 1998 by Donald Rawley
Cover photograph by Christopher Irion
Inside back cover author photograph by Roger James
Interior design by Kellan Peck
Published by arrangement with the author
ISBN: 0-380-79584-1
www.avonbooks.com/bard

Library of Congress Cataloging in Publication Data:
Rawley, Donald, 1957–
   The night bird cantata / Donald Rawley.
      p.   cm.
   I. Title.
PS3568.A846N5   1998   97-44611
813'.54—dc21   CIP

First Bard Trade Paperback Printing: June 1999
First Bard Hardcover Printing: July 1998

BARD TRADEMARK REG. U.S. PAT. OFF. AND IN OTHER COUNTRIES, MARCA REGISTRADA, HECHO EN U.S.A.

Printed in the U.S.A.

OPM 10 9 8 7 6 5 4 3 2 1

For Leonard, and Ginger, John and CCH

ACKNOWLEDGMENTS

I would like to thank my agent Noah Lukeman; my editor Jennifer Hershey for believing in my work; Kate Braverman, my first, and finest teacher, and also my dear friend, Renee Vogel, my first and on-going editor.

THE NIGHT BIRD CANTATA

{ *o n e* }

It was the summer of my mother's second husband. It was the summer of full moons, night birds and paralyzed daylight; I discovered absence and the magic of pain, gifts only the unloved can unwrap and save as something precious.

I stayed with Betty and Frank on a screened back porch with red sheets on the sleeper sofa and my own television. Betty was my grandmother's maid. She and her husband, who worked the day shift hosing down the embalming room at an all-black mortuary, welcomed me with no rules. They tried their best to make a white boy feel comfortable; in return I was expected to go out and play, run, stay up at night. I was to be a boy, something I had never thought of, and it was an intoxication.

There had been a scent of man drifting through my

mother's hair for almost six months. She smiled with a slow, backwards shimmer, talking to me as though I were one of the poodles. When I asked questions, she assumed a high, squeaky, singsong voice that she used to avoid telling me anything. My mother knew how to avoid. She had charm. It was a gift.

In turn, I did my best to stay as far away from her as I could. I was no longer in control. Her lipstick became bright with purpose. She walked ahead of me, never looking around to see if I was there. She had even called me by someone else's name, and didn't blush when she realized her mistake. I was an only child, and suddenly I found myself not part of Mama's plans.

My mother married a timid Irishman that summer. His name was Bob Rafferty, and I referred to him as ha-ha Rafferty. The name made me laugh. He was tall and blue-eyed, with dense black hair, and white, pallid skin that stretched itself over a muscular body. Bob was poor. My mother loved poor men. They married on a foggy day in June, at a wedding chapel in San Diego, not far from the Mexican border.

Perhaps it was high tide when she looked into Bob's average eyes and said she would love him and live with him. I imagined a smell of salt cross over them, the intense Pacific sun browning their faces and waves crashing on combed beaches, the big waves that carry children like me far away, into nets of seaweed and cold water.

I did not understand. I suddenly had to put my life to reason. I lost my stutter, grew tanned, hairless legs and absorbed new words like escape, flight, darkness.

It was my summer, the one I would be able to remember, and the summer whose details would be perfected into something rational and kind, as if by apology. I would be held to this distinct time, my childhood squandered except for this one memory; three months of days whose clarity is both perverse and frightening, held without photographs or postcards or any other telling semblance to prove I existed, there, in Phoenix in 1968, and that I survived.

Phoenix was the balm, the nothingness, the last stop. Powdered with midwestern money, it hid ancient people ridding themselves of tuberculosis and asthma in air-conditioned adobes with pruned cacti. Their children and grandchildren grew up wicked and full of air.

It was a new city, wrapped in construction dust. The Valley of the Sun was full of Sunday deceits and Methodist church bells. Here inconceivable clouds rolled in a huge pulse over the desert, making us small, unrewarded, powerless. The heat began in April, calculated as an assassination, and lasted through haunted summers until November.

The earth in Phoenix was infertile, smothered with cow dung and irrigation canals, making oranges grow, and grapefruit, and endless fields of flowering stock. Fuchsias, pinks and narcissus were tended by Japanese families who kept to themselves. From the road I saw their straw hats flapping in the singed wind, dipping down, then up again, into a candy floss of petals, stretched like silk toward southern mountains. The air was a stink of honey bees and wasps. When the winds shifted, these perfumes could circle me ten miles away.

In the flicker and hiss of air conditioners, night-lit golf ranges, and tiki torches glowing by Hawaiian restaurants, I grew teeth, long eyelashes, and a soft, feminine voice. It was a voice formed by incongruity and solitude; how the deck is shuffled and dealt to effeminate boys every day. How they grow up understanding the nature of sunlight, places to hide.

I swam when I was four. My grandfather threw me into the shallow end of a pool. He said swim. I went down, then came up like a dog and paddled. I never stopped swimming. I was alone and loved the feeling of emerging through that thin line which separates water and air, of repeating these elements until I collapsed on pink poolside cement, exhausted, rolling in a watery puddle to keep from burning my skin.

I ran through Phoenix lawns reeking of cottonseed and mulch, for my first ten years, on toe like a ballerina. I ran on Nogales tar roads built by clean brown men in white cotton shirts. Highways were sloped into an infirm desert. Sometimes coral and phosphorescent orange, this dry, washed land was my best friend, and I knew it by instinct; how to never be lost. The idea of being lost was a terror, and every month a new road challenged me.

I voyaged under date palms and olive trees, just beyond those brown men with their maps, shovels, and crucifixes from Spain, their wives in Tucson and Taxco, their half-breed sons. At noon things became quiet. It was the silence of a city being born, where dust-coated flowers die in full bloom and the sun sets in amethyst smoke.

*   *   *

In 1968 I believed in gods and goddesses, vampires, werewolves, and fate. I believed, as my grandmother did, in the daily horoscope, the power of numbers. I knew some part of me would grow into a beautiful, sophisticated woman, a movie star, much more important and much prettier than either my grandmother or my mother.

Questions about my future became statements. I only had to choose demands, accusations, threats I heard daily and turn them into fate. I knew none of them lasted. But surviving the day to day, the small things, that was painful. And for that I had constant questions.

The Indian women of Phoenix had answers for every question I could possibly ask and they weren't going to tell me. Answers for why I couldn't sleep, watching the moon rise through dull brown nights, my face framed by dried palm fronds and giant oleander bushes lit blue by automatic yard lights. Why none of the boys ever kept me as a friend. Why girls seemed jealous of me even though I worshipped and copied them.

These Navajo women went everywhere. They brought omens with them like transparent baggage. I saw how they were always a mile ahead of twisters, rain clouds, anything dangerous, their velvet skirts rippling in the wind.

I followed these women whenever I could. Their eyes took my small, wrinkled hands in, without questions or prayers. They had huge squash blossoms and wore city clothes of gold threads and Mexican pink cotton. I imagined they threw Kachinas in fires and spit at bugs, killing them. They made popovers in vacant, sandy lots, rolling them in honey and corn.

I found these women in back of gritty movie palaces built in the twenties, sitting hunched in shade and cooking over charcoals hurriedly thrown on cement. They offered me a hot dog, roast corn, iced tea. But always quickly, before matinees inside broke, and cars would be reparked. Before the police or theater managers could see. Before their white coals crumbled and scattered in the desert air.

Betty was high yellow and thin as her husband Frank was massive and dark. She smoked Kools by the case and her tidy, south of the river bungalow was mentholated by day and skewered with the odor of chicken and beer at night. She was proud of her furniture, all of it oriental and done up in serious purple silk. Betty covered it with tight, slippery plastic, and I liked to sit on top of her best sofa, then slide down its slick cushions and land on the floor.

Her walls were mauve, dotted with smoked mirror paste-ups instead of paintings. One smoked mirror flower, larger than me, reflected the room above the sofa. Smaller flowers floated by it, cascading into the dining room, an early Pompeii showcase with plaster marble columns and a statue of Venus near the kitchen door.

Betty loved her dolls, which hung in her second bedroom, on racks made of pressed wood. They looked like mannequin babies. Their punctured faces and bee-stung lips leered above tattered lace and Countries of the

World outfits. She was particularly proud of her Swedish dolls, and she stroked their hair for me, murmuring how beautiful this pure blond hair was, all of it real, not the plastic hair on Barbie dolls. I avoided the room at all times.

She had small collections of precious, abandoned things, discarded for something new, something better, and I didn't realize, that summer, I was one of them. The only difference was that I would be given back.

Every Sunday before church, Betty showed me her hats, each in their own pink or purple sateen box. I explained we were Catholic and my grandmother never wore hats to church, and Betty explained that in her church, all the colored ladies wore their best hats. This selection was a ritual and a chance to remember other days, when she was on the road, before Frank. Her hats were hard and crinkled, covered with grapes and peacock feathers and faded yellow lace. Betty kept a diary of which one she wore to church each Sunday.

"That one there, L.P. Your grandmother gave me that one. She wore it to Truman's inauguration. They was good friends, you know. They *were* good friends. Not was. Now why did I do that? It's Frank's fault, it is."

As my grandmother went to church once a year, and my mother never went, I came to identify the wearing of hats with devotion and pure spirituality, the most religious hats being the ones with the most feathers. That summer I noticed it took a lot of planning and effort to wear a big hat to church. You had to make sure the people in back of you could see the preacher and, according to Betty, you couldn't wear a hat more than three times the same year.

Betty looked pretty with her hair tightly pinned under hat and veil. Mysterious. She still had the old marcelled look and it tightly framed her high-cheeked, smooth mocha face. Her lips were glossed a liver red, even when she cleaned my grandmother's apartment. It was a funny, ugly brown she said was appropriate for colored women. Everything had to be appropriate and fine, that was another word. She had yellow-green eyes, a slight widow's hump, and tiny, proud feet. Her arms were long and beautifully out of proportion to the rest of her. When she cleaned for my grandmother, high up on the ninth floor, or worked in her own garden, I watched with a certain awe. Her arms blew about like silk curtains in a wind.

Frank was a blue-black giant, whose skin manufactured its own oil, like a Texas field. I reasoned he could eat a whole pot of ants and never jump up or wiggle. When he walked, metal chimed and furniture seemed to rearrange itself. His massive shoulders constantly burst the seams of his fine, church Sunday suit, a sharkskin with a subtle stripe. Betty spent one day out of every month repairing it with a silver thread she said came from a good white store in Hollywood. When Frank put his suit on, Betty mumbled to herself that Frank would bust it by noon.

"Where's Frank, L.P.?" Betty had selected a hat and put the other boxes carefully away in her bedroom closet.

My name was, and still is, L.P., short for Lindsay Paul,

from my great grandfather. It could have been a girl's name, which was fine by me, as I had always wanted to be a girl. A very pretty girl. I didn't realize I wasn't until my fourth birthday, when I received a catcher's mitt from one of mother's boyfriends. I didn't know what it was. He looked at me and asked, with a heavy animal laugh, if I was a girl. I said yes, and gave him back the mitt. He never called my mother after that.

"L.P.! You in back?" I could hear Betty's voice in her bedroom. It was lazy, unfocused. I was watching *Batman* on the porch.

"Dammit! L.P.!" Betty's voice changed an octave. My mother told me to be polite to Betty, so I got up and went to her door.

"Yes, Betty." When I saw her in the half-light of her shuttered purple bedroom, she looked like a shiny demon in her satin slip. Her hump made a slight arch and I saw she had hair under her arms, something I had never seen before, and I was fascinated. Betty took two small pads and put them under each arm. Once in place, she sprayed herself with a perfume called "White Witch," with a label that read "KINGSTON, JAMAICA." It smelled like old rich women.

"L.P., if Frank's not here you'll have to zip me up for church."

I was annoyed. If I had to zip her up, that meant I had to get dressed, and there was still two good hours of Sunday morning television. They showed *Heckle and Jeckle* on Sunday morning.

"But church isn't until one, Betty. It's only ten." I waited for her reaction.

Betty lit a Kool and French inhaled. Her eyes had become alert, greener in the purple light than they would be in the sun.

"No matter. You know I like to be prepared. You got to be prepared in life, L.P. Be ready early. Besides, it's Christ's Day and I don't want to walk around my house in a slip on a Sunday. It's not appropriate, L.P."

"Yes, Betty." My voice was reasonable. I hoped she didn't know I was staring at her armpits.

She motioned for me to zip her up, and I yanked the zipper as best I could, then knew I had to be a little more tender around the hump. Betty couldn't fasten the hook so I did.

"You're turning into quite a gentleman for just ten, L.P." Halfway down, she stubbed her cigarette out and lit another. Betty watched me as I turned to go into the hall.

"You going to see Grover and Samuel in church today?" Betty's words made me stop.

"Sure. I guess." I liked Grover and Samuel, but more important, they liked me. Grover was blue-black, a little lighter than Frank, and was Marcelline's son. Marcelline wore false eyelashes and had enormous titties. She was president of the Colored Ladies Bowling League of South Phoenix. Grover was heavy, never going out for sports or physical exercise, but he could sure lift his bowling ball at his mother's tournaments. When his ball rolled in the gutter Marcelline would roll her eyes, yell out zero and pop the cap off another beer. Sometimes he scored big. Strikes. Eights and nines. And Marcelline still rolled her eyes.

Samuel was the only Negro boy I met who wore glasses and had to keep his hair crew cut like mine. We both hated it. None of the boys liked him because he wore glasses, and they told him he looked like a white boy, so he became my friend. Samuel was a runt like me. And he also believed he was a girl.

I met them a year before my summer with Betty, on a day of lilacs and graves. Frank was being paid overtime to help out with a funeral, and came home with arms full of white lilies and lilacs for Betty. I was spending the night with them, as my mother had a date and my grandparents were out of town.

Marcelline, Doris, and Betty were having margaritas and gin stingers in her purple living room. The air conditioner was on, spraying an ice over the women, who were drunk and laughing in slow, escalating threads of hoarse whispers and cackles. They were talking about men.

Grover and Samuel and I were placed in the backyard and told to get along. High clouds had turned the sky into an oiled, hot pearl and we couldn't find a shadow anywhere.

We didn't realize we were the shadows, stuck outside and told to get along. There were simply too many facets to the adult world, and for me it was easy to find the shadows. To sink back, disappear. Which was what I was trying to do in Betty's hall, but she would have none of it.

"You wear the nice bow tie your mama left you to wear in church." Betty crossed her arms and stood in front of me. The pinpoint of her spike heel tapped the floor.

"It's hot." I backed away. I had been with Betty only two weeks and already I had to wear bow ties and go to church. But many things made up for it. Betty let me stay up until I fell asleep. It made me feel normal, as I had a sleeping disorder. Now I knew when I fell asleep I wouldn't wake up until morning.

Betty turned and pinned me with her eyes. She was attaching earrings to her ears, and they seemed to hurt.

"And?" She wasn't going to wait for my reply.

I nodded my head that I would wear the tie, and went back to the television. I saw Betty staring at me, then at the television. She was all put together, and had a margarita in her hand. Betty always felt it appropriate to have a drink before church. Made her sing better. Because that's what she was. A singer.

"You want to see something, L.P.? We got some time to kill."

I had missed almost twenty minutes of *Heckle and Jeckle* and I was furious. But I knew I had to be on my best behavior. All summer. Betty motioned for me to follow her into the bedroom again. She pulled out another hatbox from her closet and patted the bed. I sat next to her, looking at the embroidered pink roses on her coat, which she kept on in the house. It looked just like a coat Jackie Kennedy wore.

"I found these when I was looking at my hats." Betty smiled. I realized she was speaking not to me but to her purple bedroom.

Inside her hatbox were old black-and-white photographs wrapped in tissue paper. Betty played in a band in the late thirties and wore flowered dresses to the floor, flowers in her hair, flowers on her bosom and wrists. She didn't have a hump then.

"Look, L.P. This was me in Harlem in 1942, before the war ended. I met Frank when he returned, at a party here. But that was way later. Do you know who that was?"

Betty pointed to a fat man with bulging eyes, holding a trumpet.

"That's Louis Armstrong. He bought me coffee once when I did a radio show in Philadelphia. Do you know where Philadelphia is?"

Betty studied me. Her question was nice. I wasn't sure where Philadelphia was.

"Kinda."

The bulging eyed man's photograph fluttered down into the box. Another took its place. A picture of Betty in front of a microphone as big as her face. She was skinny then. Her face seemed transfixed, eyes glassy and frank as greasy quarters. She was singing in black and white, not color, and I sensed that black-and-white sound was scratched. Clarinets and saxophones hid something warped. But she was glamorous. Her rhinestone earrings were long, brushing her shoulders, and her shoulders were powdered to make her look white.

"Philadelphia is where I was born, L.P. It's a big old town with pretty buildings and the Constitution. They're nice to coloreds there."

Then a picture of Betty in front of an enormous black

car, holding a Chihuahua. There were palms and orange trees in the distance.

"Where's that?" I looked up at Betty. She winced.

"That's Hollywood, honey. See, when I stopped singing . . ."

"Why did you stop singing?" I didn't realize I was asking the wrong questions.

"Because I said the wrong thing to someone, L.P. So I moved to Hollywood."

"Is that where people go who say the wrong things?" This was a revelation to me. Perhaps there was a place for me. I said the wrong things all the time. Perhaps there was a place for boys who thought they were girls, shy people, skinny people who couldn't fight, people who searched for shadows on high cloud days.

Betty stared at her picture, trying to see something in it. I studied it too. The afternoon light in the picture made a thin, opaque white light around Betty, and everything in the picture seemed so clear and focused, like photographs of presidents standing in front of ships and meeting royalty. I wondered if everyone in Hollywood, those people like me who left because they said the wrong things, walked around with this silver light attached to them, like close-ups on old thirties films. I knew the light protected them. It made them happy.

Suddenly I realized someone important didn't like Betty. I thought, how could anyone not like Betty? The midmorning sun pulsed through thin rows of dust in the purple bedroom.

Betty caught her breath and tapped the picture.

"That was my Chihuahua. Just like Billie Holiday."
She smiled.

"Who was Billie Holiday, Betty?"

"She was Lady Day." The finality in her voice signaled me not to ask any further.

"Did you like Hollywood?" I certainly liked the idea of big black cars and palm trees. And never saying wrong things. Being touched by white light.

Betty froze, transfixed, then smiled in an artificial way. She reminded me of my mother.

"Oh, L.P. It's quite a place. Quite a place."

"Why did you leave it, Betty? Why did you come to Phoenix? I hate Phoenix. I'll never come back when I grow up."

There was a silence. I heard the icebox hum briefly, then shut itself off. Betty's mouth turned inward. She wore false teeth, and she suddenly touched them, pushing them up, and checked her fingers to make sure there was no lipstick.

"Someday you'll know why. There's no point explaining it to you now. Frank's still not home. I have to get him to church."

Betty quietly put the lid back on her hatbox. She sipped her margarita and waved me out of her purple realm. She didn't bustle around that day when Frank came home. She just told him to get ready, the suit's fixed, and she stayed in her bedroom, smoking cigarette after cigarette.

When Frank finally came in, I had put on my bow tie, hating it. Frank put a massive hand on my head, on the top, where my cowlick was. His eyes were very white, like fresh cream, and he smelled like Jockey Club.

"Where's Betty?" I asked, looking through the Italian ruins of the dining room.

"Betty's getting herself done up. You know how she gets funny." His voice became lower.

"We got to be men and be nice to Betty today. It's Sunday." Frank considered this a pronouncement, and I stared out the window at a row of oak and eucalyptus trees. They were quite still. Why did we always have to be men? Wouldn't it be nice to be girls, too? I was annoyed, but nodded my head.

Soon Betty came out, and Frank put his beer down. Her hat had a white veil with wide netting and tiny birds fastened at the border, flying against her cheek. She had red eyes and seemed clumsy, and I realized, as did Frank, that Betty was drunk.

BETTY COULDN'T KEEP a garden, but she tried. The backyard of her bungalow bred desert weeds and gophers, and nervous lines of rose bushes with crisp flowers. By a chain-link fence in back, a date palm that had never been trimmed sported dead fronds, reaching down like a beard to the nape of its trunk. Here Betty had planted miniature peach trees that scraped the ground, and tomatoes and pumpkin squash.

Her bulldog, Brenda, was kept outside in a tin lean-to. Brenda had a white spot on her chest that Betty said was a star, a sign of good breeding. Brenda had horrifying breath, and killed much of the garden with her urine. She was bathed every Saturday, in early evening, and Brenda loved Frank more than she loved Betty. I liked Brenda, but she stayed far away from me after sniffing me. Brenda didn't like the smell of white people.

On that back porch with rusted screens, I watched tomatoes and roses grow and quickly die. I regretted little. Nights were an unsprung blue, a coiled indigo that shimmered with heat. Fireflies were rare in Phoenix, but Betty had them in that tenacious, angry little garden. They stayed close to Betty and Frank's sharp, cheap grass, occasionally flying up and twirling down when their altitudes burned them.

The television was full of summer programs, old movies, Wallace and Ladmo, Vietnam, Batman, and the Supremes. I wrote poems about seagulls, because I hadn't seen any. I drank beer and Hi-C punch from a cooler. It was the first time I drank beer, and I drank it all summer, drunk and skinny and shy, my weaving silhouette taunting the Phoenix dusk, its violent fire a lingering net of cumulus clouds and dust.

Betty called those Phoenix sunsets the blood of the afternoon, and there is no sun like a Phoenix sun. I believed all sunsets anywhere in the world were just like Phoenix; pure as a trance, its electric colors descending like angels into black palms and rocks.

I took salt tablets during the day and a cold shower at night, or my sinuses would inflame and I would faint. Betty always had my salt tablets ready with breakfast, sometimes even a snitch of beer from the night before. Had my mother known, she would have fired Betty. I felt I had a friend.

It was that day, getting ready for church, in the second week of a baked June, with Betty drunk in her purple bedroom, waiting for Frank, fastening tiny, real feathered birds to netting yellow with nicotine, I remembered a day when I'd learned something about Betty and Hollywood.

My eyes were too large and I was an easy read. My grandmother told me my eyes reminded her of Judy Garland and Olivia de Havilland. Betty agreed with her, having worked in Hollywood as a nanny. It was as though her having spent time in Hollywood made Betty an expert on things glamorous. My grandmother and Betty sat in the kitchen discussing news of the stars as Betty washed the dishes and nodded, agreeing every time, just to keep the conversation going.

My grandmother's kitchen wasn't particularly large, as it was an apartment, but it had a quality about it that encouraged conversation. A table and four well-upholstered French chairs, done in tartan. Everything necessary for life on this kitchen table: salt, pepper, mustard, ketchup, sugar, Diet Rite Cola, crackers, paper napkins, and magazines; all of which were crammed onto a lazy susan in the center of the table. This way my grandmother could walk into the kitchen and stay there, next to Betty, food, and the phone. Until noon, when she put herself together.

I was in the living room. My grandfather was off on his daily walk, the cane he bought in Havana helping him; twice slowly around the apartment building, then once down the street in back of our apartments. My mother was at college.

My grandfather was a kind, silent, continually ill man

who had the mark and smooth demeanor of a fine gentleman. He lived to be ninety-five, in constant pain, losing limbs, fingers, in the process, as well as parts of his intestines, his hearing, and eyesight. But he had a routine. That, I determined, was why he lived so long. While he could still walk, he walked with a variety of canes, some with silver owl tips, or carved alligators and parrots, handpainted with the words HAVANA or KEY WEST.

People would wave to my grandfather on his half-hour, midmorning walks. The doormen, gardeners, and delivery men at our apartment building waved. The doctors getting out of their Lincolns with suicide doors, at the medical plaza next door, waved. They used to check their wristwatches and shake their heads. Henry Adams was always on time.

My grandfather read the *Wall Street Journal* and the Phoenix papers every morning, then retreated to his bathroom to do, as he called it, his toilette. When he finally went blind, he simply substituted an hour-long morning news program on CBS radio, *Radio to the World*, and listened to that with the same calm efficiency he had when reading. When he lost half a leg at the age of ninety-four from diabetes, strokes, and sheer age, my grandmother, in one of the few kind gestures of her life, constructed a wrap-around bed tray for his needs.

At the end, my grandfather had a small, transistor radio which no one touched but him. My grandmother told my mother that before he died, in those last days of shut silk curtains, day nurses, and the stink of already dead skin, she knew he was alert because she heard the transistor radio being turned on full volume for perhaps a minute, then turned off. This occurred twice a day, once midmorning, then at six.

It was better than checking a pulse, my grandmother said. One day, in a top floor hotel suite in Washington, D.C., in the middle of a damp summer, the radio didn't come on. My grandmother said later she understood the silence, and immediately called her lawyer.

My grandmother was my mother and my mother was my sister; telling me to stay by her side, against the witch, my grandmother. We lived with my grandparents, Georgia and Henry Adams Fowler, in a ritzy pink apartment building in Phoenix, on Central Avenue. The building had ground quartz mixed in the cement, and when the sun hit it at midafternoon, it sparkled.

My mother and I lived in a two-bedroom apartment on the third floor, with a view of a dirt lot and twenty-four date palms that I counted each morning. It made my world congruous and safe. If there were still twenty-four palms when I woke up, then we would still be allowed to live there, without fighting and recriminations, under the auspices of my grandmother, Georgia, who never failed to remind me that my mother could never give me this lifestyle. And how lucky and smart I would be.

My grandmother was a tarantula in mink. Her huge, blue apartment was crammed with forty years of French furniture, Mexican blown glass from Tijuana and Nogales, ornate gilt mirrors from Spain, and silvery bedrooms with silk-canopied beds.

The air was kept constantly cool because Georgia said it was a healthier temperature, and that Phoenix's heat never agreed with her. The only reason she was here was my grandfather's heart problems and asthma, and she remarked that all the women she associated with were in the same fix. Each had a sick, old husband. Each woman would have preferred to be in Manhattan, Miami, San Francisco, or Washington, D.C. But they had to make do with the desert.

These rooms on the ninth floor, my grandmother's arena, stank of her perfume, "JeReviens" by Worth, and even though she had hundreds of bottles, lined up like trophies, she only wore one. Yet these perfumes stood like skyscrapers in Louis XV vitrines with emaciated, curved legs, and paintings of men with buckled shoes and tights, playing harps and lyres. She only wore Worth because, as she pointed out to me one day, women should choose one scent and never vary. Women of quality are known for the way they smell.

She also pointed out I would be made fun of, that people would be jealous of me, that there was no love in this world. After forty years with my grandfather, she realized there wasn't love, only need and compliance. Sexual love dies in a day. I tried to form the word "compliance" on my lips and it came out "cmplernce." I used every word I heard her say.

Georgia had bought three apartments in this costume jewel of a building, with its fool's gold walls and swimming pool and gardens. Each was an odd number and each apartment a different color. Georgia believed in the numbers, in horses, odds on cards, colors, and the zodiac.

Her apartment was a weapon of French blue. It was everywhere: the carpet, walls, upholstery, tablecloths. The apartment faced east and in the afternoon this wondrous cave turned a lavender. I would stare out at Camelback Mountain and Paradise Valley, and dance with myself. I was Sophia Loren. I was traveling in a plane and I was on my way to Rome.

There was a third apartment, on the seventh floor, to use for storage. Georgia came here from a twenty-seven-room house in Washington, D.C., something she never let me forget, and she kept every item that crossed her path. This apartment on the seventh floor was a sea-mist green made darker by heavy curtains cooling it from the dry torture of Phoenix's squalid afternoons. Here furniture and boxes were packed to the ceiling in all rooms.

I knew that in this tomb there were horrors waiting for me; dead bodies lay wrapped in satin comforters, in the arctic dark of the guest bedroom. There, dead people sat on the toilets in pitch-black, pink-tiled bathrooms. In the living room they hid, dead and wet, behind double-stacked sofas, boxes of pillows and empty liquor decanters, plastic philodendrons, the blown glass horses and eagles. I refused to go through the front door.

It was in this series of rooms held in the sky, filled with colors and desert and hatred, that I learned to listen in. I was always kept at arm's length, told about manners, and stunted, as only someone with a dwarf's heart can be.

I could hear Betty distinctly. Her voice in the kitchen was in sync with her day: gossipy, deferential, relaxed.

"Yes, Miss Georgia. I knew Liz Taylor was no good.

When I worked for the Flynns back when she was just a sprite, she was already drinking and all."

"Really." Georgia's eyes narrowed and she crossed her legs with a heave. She sipped her Diet Rite Cola. This was a ritual, a six-pack a day, then coffee with dinner, pacing her rooms like a lioness. These rooms contained her life and her disappointments, like a being waiting for yet another method of deliverance. From fate when it decides to be lousy and real.

"She's got damn nice eyes, Betty." Georgia leaned her head back against the kitchen wall, a common gesture my mother hated. Mother said it made Georgia look like a cowboy.

My grandmother had a way of being extremely crude in all matters relating to men and sex.

"So how was he in the sack?" was Georgia's first response to my mother when she spoke of going out on a date.

"Did you get there?" my grandmother would ask, lowering her lids. My mother never could handle my grandmother when she began to discuss matters sexual.

In anything else, Georgia's voice became smooth, sophisticated, with a light Southern lisp.

I positioned myself at a corner of the dining room so I could see in without them knowing. My grandmother sighed, then continued talking to Betty in a friendly, girlish voice.

"But then, my eyes are just as good. I came out like a bandit, didn't I?" Georgia waited for the correct reply.

"You sure did, Miss Georgia. You have such pretty things."

From the ninth floor, Georgia stared out at the indecent desert below, spotted with citrus groves and walled-in houses that tried to be Spanish. After movies, Georgia found little to discuss except one thing.

"You ever hear about that little Flynn boy, Betty?"

"No ma'am. Never will. My heart broke."

Betty stopped, stared at my grandmother for a precise, dramatic moment. She wiped her hands with a towel and left the kitchen for a hall closet and the vacuum cleaner. I raced back to my original spot, then drifted into the kitchen after Betty went into another room.

My grandmother began to apply her lipstick after Betty's exit, a callous, comfortable gesture, and I realized the two women were beginning their separate days.

I couldn't reason why my grandmother had been cruel.

"Nana, why is Betty upset? What did you say?"

"I beg your pardon?" She stopped her lipstick, looking up at me from over the lazy susan.

"You were mean to Betty." I looked at the floor.

"I wasn't being mean, L.P. Honestly." She was annoyed. I was becoming too precocious. Georgia smacked her lips against a paper napkin, her gaze intent on a pearl-and-gold pocket mirror. She spoke quietly.

"See, you come in and say something like that, I know you've been eavesdropping. There are things you don't know. Betty raised Errol Flynn's son. You know who Errol Flynn was?"

"No." I breathed in deep.

"Well, honey, he was the biggest movie star in the world. And handsome. My kind of man, L.P. Betty did a good job. I saw it on her references. She's been with us since you were a baby. You know that?" Georgia's eyes became sharp.

I nodded my head and watched my grandmother. She looked back at her mirror. Her beige-blond hair was swept up in a messy chignon, which she began to straighten. Her face was carefully powdered, eyebrows plucked, and rouge neatly brushed on her upper cheeks. Her gray eyes were electric. She never stopped reminding me that my eyes, although brown, were the same as hers. That we were lucky to be living with my grandfather and her, because my mother was an idiot. A girl who wasn't very smart and never would be. But I was. I could read and write when I was three. I was just like her.

"It was real sad, honey. Here this little boy grows up and Betty thinks he's her own. He goes into the U.S. Army, and the next thing you know he's lost in Vietnam. Betty was so sad she tried to kill herself. Ever notice how funny her wrists are?"

"Yes."

"Well, there you are." Georgia smirked. "In my day it would have been off to the funny farm with her. She recovered quick."

"Why?" I didn't understand why anyone who was sad would have to be put away.

"She tried to slit her wrists, L.P. It's a crime. Let all her colored blood go right down the toilet. Now you understand me?"

My grandmother frightened me when she spoke this way. She talked like Barbara Stanwyck: her lips and teeth clenched, words escaping in a poisonous fume. It was tough and cold and unwarranted, but Georgia knew how to underscore, show everything hideous under the beauty, and this was just one of her talents. She *knew* what was ugly.

She gave Betty beautiful clothes, like acetate satin coats with New York labels, and caftans, and hats. She gave Betty and Frank money at Christmas, Thanksgiving, and Easter, plus dinnerware and sets of old crystal she'd find in her seventh-floor tomb, but she talked about colored people as though they were as stupid as her only daughter. She said they were children. Savages.

I realized perhaps I was the new baby to Betty, but she always looked at me with a strange glint in her face, like I was a picture in a magazine.

"If it makes her so sad, then why?" I couldn't finish my thought.

Georgia tapped her stoplight-red nails on her kitchen table and continued in her steady, hushed, behind-closed-doors voice.

"It's what makes her special. See, L.P., everyone's got something that makes them special."

"She almost cried," I realized.

"Betty loves to talk about it. You wouldn't understand." Suddenly I was angry at being told I wouldn't understand. My voice became low and it surprised me.

"Then what makes you so special?" I dared to ask.

Georgia gave me a half smile and took her concentration away from the compact. She took in a deep breath, then pulled out her pouch of jewelry from her purse. She did this every day, before she put on her clothes, and always in the kitchen. Face and jewelry first, then her clothes. My grandmother attached herself to life, gold, and lipstick first.

Fastening gold chains around her neck, wrists, and fingers, Georgia became rueful, incandescent.

"I'm special because I'm rich. I'm still young and pretty. And I'm a smart businesswoman, L.P. Why, in Washington, D.C., I was friends to three First Ladies, and let me tell you something else; they still send me birthday cards. *Not* Christmas cards, *everybody* gets Christmas cards from the White House. But those girls remember my birthday and that, L.P., is special. That is how you become special. Any nigger can work for a movie star."

My grandmother chuckled to herself. She popped open another can of Diet Rite and dismissed me. I wanted to cry, but I knew Betty might be in the next room. I wondered if she had heard. I didn't look for her in that huge, ninth-floor cage. I sat down at my grandmother's rococo baby grand piano, stared out at Camelback Mountain, and touched its keys, trying to make the sound as soft as I could, blue and low in the air.

three

ON THE WAY to church, I began to feel extremely warm with my clip-on bow tie, and snuck it off in the back-seat. Frank drove in silence, taking curves with one huge hand on the steering wheel. His nails were clean; Betty insisted they be clean for church, but I could smell bleach and something else. Embalming fluid.

Betty was half asleep, her shoulders and head lightly rolling to the rhythm of the car. The windows in the car were down, and I liked the way the hot June air blew on my face until I couldn't think. I watched Betty's carefully arranged miniature birds flutter around her jaw, then slowly come to rest as Frank hit the stoplight.

Phoenix was a segregated city. Colored people lived south of the Gila River, a dry, shabby canal, only good for floods. It served as a dividing line, its bleached, sharp rocks carefully strung as barbed wire. I never knew there was a South Phoenix until I visited Betty, then stayed with her that summer. South Phoenix was invisible because it was black.

Here, houses were small, squatting in dry grass like nesting hens. But there were surprisingly tall, rich trees offering a broad shade, moving with sun, scooping sandy earth into a continuous sundial. Cars were stripped, left roadside, and their tires and hubcaps and bumpers were made into pots for vegetables and corn.

Indians were not welcome here, and I concurred if they were, things would have had more color, been prettier, with wagon wheels and feathers in front of shops.

Further south, past the cement block bungalows with air coolers on their roofs, were the flower fields. The Japanese families were also not welcome, and did their shopping and business in their own town, which had ten or twelve buildings with flared roofs, painted gold, that glowed in the sun.

I knew after church we would go bowling. Betty had my day, as every day this summer, taped on her refrigerator in a scrawl of pencil and crayon; if I didn't want to do something, all I had to do was change it by running a line through, and she never said a word. As the summer became stoic and exhausted by heat, the things I had to do, the plans on that refrigerator door, became less and less.

I realized Betty always explained to me what I had to do to get through life, at least for that day. It was something my grandmother and mother couldn't be bothered with. Their vision for themselves was far too grand to be dealt with on a daily basis, and I realized that even before I lived with her, it had been Betty I would come to when I was confused.

Frank barely touched the steering wheel with his left hand. We seemed to float in the Phoenix summer, the wind and dry heat not allowing us conversation, or smiles. Going to church with feathers, silk suits, bow ties, and birds. I reasoned, watching Betty's head bob in a stupor, that we had taken the time to show God we cared. He would fulfill our prayers because we were dressed up.

There wasn't much Betty could tell me now. No answers or sensible justifications for childhood. She had an answer for anything I asked, but that was my white world, and one easily deciphered.

In this other place, Betty became female, an incarnation of things made from velvet, used only once. Betty seemed to adopt the stance of those who suffer, who breathe out to relax, but wind up coughing, those who are not quite sure, those who retreat.

I promised myself to ask Betty, later in our days and months, if passing a river changes perspective. If people with darker skins create a denser, more incoherent air. If blood changes its rhythm. If I could become a woman, simply by being.

When I was five I asked Betty questions.

"Are you a hundred years old?" I asked, watching her clean my grandmother's chandelier. She was on a ladder and I could see tiny broken veins around her ankles. I had a cherry Popsicle in my mouth.

"Older," she whispered to me. I sat numb for a day.

In the kitchen, after my grandmother went shopping up Central Avenue, Betty stood by the kitchen sink, lit a Kool, and polished Georgia's endless cache of silver, most of it inexpensive, but kept highly polished at all times.

"Shit goddamn."

"What does shit goddamn mean, Betty?"

"It means silver polish smells, L.P."

She was right. I watched tarnish wipe off through a cloud of ammonia. There were felt runners to stack the platters. It all had to be put away with soft boards and round felt pads that folded into half-moons. I thought they were the most useless things I'd ever seen. I told Betty she should throw them away, and she shook her head no, stubbing her cigarette out, and immediately lit another.

"Your grandmama would have a pissin' fit, L.P. Certain things have to have certain things to take care of them. Make sure they don't bust." Betty slid a pad between two silver plates.

"They look like Frisbees, but you can't throw them." I didn't buy her reasoning. That was the beginning of my willingness to discard. I collect everything, even people, and discard them. If something doesn't make sense to me, then I throw it away.

Betty had dark hands. There were two bubbly pink lines across her wrists. I assumed, at the age of five, that she spent a great deal of time in the sun. I loved to watch her hands glide over wood sideboards and my grandmother's huge, round onyx cocktail table. It was made in Mexico, but resembled a Chinese coin, and had an underside of smoked glass. I crawled around under the cocktail table until Betty found me one afternoon.

"L.P., what are you doing?" I could hear the flat monotone of Betty's voice. I knew I had to think quick.

"I'm in my house," I pleaded, "it's mine and you can't have it."

"L.P., dogs crawl under furniture. Not you. What would your nana or your mama do if they saw you? Get out from under there!" As I did, I bumped my head on the onyx. Outside, cumulus clouds stained the sky with shadow and cotton. The apartment passed into a momentary darkness. I looked up at Betty and she seemed suddenly delicate, the clouds' shadows passing over her like melanoma crawling rapidly up a leg.

Blue, dark French gray-blue. Betty's eyes were wide and I saw a yellowish rim on one. She seemed so brown. She stood completely still in her white uniform, watching the storm from the ninth floor. She held a vase from Tijuana that Georgia had bought for a dollar and put next to a Sèvres urn.

"I like thunder," I whispered.

"I don't," Betty countered, her eyes hard and foreign.

Thunder shook the apartment and I giggled. Betty almost dropped the dollar vase and quickly put it on the dining room table.

I had to ask her. It was always on my mind.

"Betty, why is your skin chocolate like those See's candies?"

Her concentration broken, she stared at me, then smiled, lit another Kool, and blew a long, luxurious mane of smoke through her nose. I could smell the menthol.

"Because I eat them all day."

"You eat chocolates all day?" I was intrigued.

"Sure do, honey. You eat enough and you'll turn chocolate, too. Your nana eats plenty. Wouldn't she be funny if she turned chocolate one day, like me? Just up and turned milk chocolate and sweet?"

Betty began to laugh through her throat. I realized she was sharing something adult with me, though I wasn't sure what it was.

"It'd be a whole new world. That I'd like to see." Shaking her head, she wiped her hands on a towel.

She shook out her feet as she laughed, something I'd never seen before, and I spent the rest of the day trying to attempt her laugh, and trying to shake my feet. I fell down twice.

When I was sick Betty fixed me soup and put a slab of butter in it, which revolted me. I put the butter under my pillow and she found its puddle the following day. She stood at the foot of my bed and glared.

"You don't like my butter? It's good for you."

There was a pause. I wasn't going to give in. Butter made me retch.

"It'll make you into a strong man." Betty waited for me to reply.

"I don't wanna. I want to be a girl."

My fever had broken, but I could hear my voice, nasal and silly, echoing inside my nose. Betty pulled the pillows from under me and began to change the pillowcases.

"Don't talk that way. That way is not natural. Besides, you're a boy."

"I am not."

Betty's head twitched as though the thought paralyzed her.

"Oh Jesus." Betty said "Jesus" a lot. I wondered if she was mad.

I was in one of my grandmother's double beds, in her guest room, which was done in heavy wood, carved with dragons and lions with claw feet. I believed at night they came alive. In the closets Georgia kept her minks and sequined dresses, and I used to open the closet doors enough that I could see them sparkle.

This was before my mother and I were given the third-floor apartment to live in. My mother was always on probation with Georgia, and had to prove her ability to please my grandmother, thus insuring us of bits and pieces. Of largesse.

I turned my face up to Betty. Her jaw seemed tight.

"Betty, are you angry?"

"No, sweetheart. I'm not angry. You're just cranky. Tired."

I realized the air had become acrid. Betty turned her face away from me, pretending to dust the vanity table. I suddenly realized she didn't want to look at me. She usually dusted the vanity table on Fridays. Today was Monday. Betty wiped her nose and started humming.

"What's that?"

"A church hymn, L.P. You like church?"

I had never liked church. Our Catholic church Sunday School was in a cold room covered with vines. It looked like a Boris Karloff movie, and I pretended I was one of those girls with long tattered evening gowns and plucked eyebrows who became zombies and threw themselves off cliffs. There was a young nun who disliked me intensely, and sent me home with a note that said I couldn't concentrate on the Bible, or hymns, and I watched too much television. That I was a destructive influence on the girls in the class. I was trying to turn them into improper young ladies.

"No."

"You'd like church. My church."

"Do you have nuns, Betty? They're mean."

Betty smiles. "No. No nuns, L.P. We're Baptists. We sing."

"I want to be Cleopatra. She didn't go to church."

Betty shook her head and sighed, keeping her eyes away from me as she fluffed my pillows.

"I think you need some of my church. You'd straighten up real quick."

"Yuck."

"That all you can say?" Her tone was fierce, and I began to giggle, an obnoxious, spoiled giggle. Betty still refused to look at me, and I quieted down.

"Do you love us, Betty?"

Silence. I became angry, as I demanded attention from her whenever we were alone together. I had decided, Cleopatra aside, that I was a beautiful movie star, maybe my favorite, Sophia Loren, and even though I was sick, I should be paid attention to.

Finally Betty turned and focused on me, even though I could see she wasn't looking at me. I couldn't comprehend what was in her eyes. They were red, and I figured she had some Phoenix dust in them, something she always complained about.

"I love you as much as I can." Betty took my bed tray and the greasy pillowcases out into the hall. I didn't understand. I wasn't expected to, and I promised myself I would understand everything people said to me when I grew up. I would never let anyone say something and just walk out of a room.

The afternoon sun came through my grandmother's Venetian blinds, and dust floated in zigzags, piercing my grandmother's blue, and I closed my eyes.

four

I WASN'T BORN in Phoenix. I was a bastard, a breech birth conceived in the back of a Chrysler in 1957 in Evanston, Illinois. The landscape of my conception was stained with gray, acid towns and grimacing highways of snow, momentarily white as a butcher's clean apron. My mother was wearing orchids on her wrists that shook like soft bells under my father. It was a night with no stars. Singed early spring blue and perfumed by frosted trees.

I was nine hours in delivery and only four and a half pounds. My mother was drugged, but she could see me, misshapen and clutching, a lousy reason for marriage to my father Leo, a Czech whom my grandmother despised for his immigrant status, his common family from a Communist country.

There were American Beauty roses in my mother's

room, from my grandmother and great grandmother, but none from my father, who was on the road selling plastics in Omaha and Dubuque and Cleveland.

My mother dreamed of blood. A sleekness of wet things that cry. There was a Chicago wind as I slept. Subject to instant fevers, I was wrapped in tinfoil and placed on ice.

We left my father when I was a year old. Dressed in a cowboy hat, I slept on the plane, not knowing then I would be held in arms of air for the rest of my life, or that sunsets and certain miracles would come to me in Phoenix. In the dry stench of the desert, children turn into travelers. As adults they never stop staring out windows, leaving first at parties, divorcing, moving between cities and losing touch. But there is always an open road waiting, and in Phoenix, the roads don't end.

At her only daughter's birth, Georgia still had enough spite left to name her baby Violet. My mother was an exact opposite of me. She weighed in at eight pounds five ounces and never stopped screaming. My grandfather was fifty and my grandmother thirty. He never expected a child so late in life, and my grandmother received a ruby and diamond bracelet upon the birth of her daughter, which she wore in the hospital and showed to all the nurses. It was 1937. Jean Harlow had just died.

The same American Beauty roses that signaled my emergence into the world were in my grandmother's hospital room, and their red petals left a scented, messy trail on the mosaic Italianate tile on the floor. My grandfather, too, was busy at his factory making the machinery that would be used in World War II to help planes carry bombs over the Atlantic, but he came late in the evening, in a three-piece silk suit and a Homburg with a clipped parrot feather on the side.

My grandfather was happy. He loved this plump, sassy little girl baby with Georgia's eyes and his head. He remarked that even only half a day old, Violet was moving her arms. A one-two punch.

My grandmother lit a cigarette, sipping on coffee. She was wearing a peignoir with white fox and had applied her makeup. My mother was eight hours old. My grandmother complained that she wanted to leave the hospital as soon as possible, she was perfectly fine. She looked at her ruby and diamond bracelet in the harsh, average light of the hospital, Violet nursing at her breast as my grandfather watched with tears in his eyes.

Quietly my grandmother put her breast back in the peignoir, lifting Violet into her lacy bassinet, and took one last drag on her cigarette, then stubbed it out, staring at my grandfather, saying only this:

"I wanted a boy."

My mother was twenty when I was born. After her divorce, Mama had nothing and my grandmother took her in, even though she felt her daughter was slow, stupid, and would never amount to much. Or what she had planned. My mother was supposed to marry an embassy man, or a senator, or a Wall Street man, not an immigrant selling plastics in the Midwest.

My grandmother told me my mother was beyond

dumb, that she considered Violet slightly retarded, which Mama wasn't, but Georgia never stopped tapping her nails on tables when my mother was around. She'd stand up, then sit down, and look around the room with ashamed eyes. Her daughter made her nervous.

Mama was never particularly pretty during her adolescence; overweight with distraught, curly hair, she was a tomboy, then a rebel, then a tramp. Only later, after I was born, did my mother become a beauty, an exceptional beauty that men stopped for. It took my grandmother by surprise and she was envious, as her looks were fabrication.

Georgia put my mother through debutante parties and finishing schools. She even bribed a judge to make my mother Miss U.S. Bonds. Violet sat on a covered wagon in the middle of Rock Creek Park, Bob Hope on one side and her and Constance Bennett on the other, smiling to an extremely small crowd. Mama was now a beauty queen. Mama was smart enough to run away.

She wound up at Northwestern University, and she explained to me that summer when she got married that Northwestern University still wasn't far enough.

When I struggled for breath outside her womb, my mother gasped; I had an extremely large head, far too large for my body, which gave me the effect of something deformed, wasted. But my face was pretty. This huge head, the doctor knew, would gradually match my body; he said at birth it could be molded into another shape if done right away. My mother murmured no, leave it. He's mine.

Her breasts were small and she didn't manufacture

milk. In my first few days I almost died from an unexplained fever. Fevers were part of my childhood, as was
time spent alone. But I had my grandmother, whom we
lived with, and I became the object of her affection
and plans.

"See all this, L.P.?" My grandmother sat at her vanity
table in her silver bedroom, near oriental rugs, a king-
sized bed with a crown, and silver-and-beige draperies
coming down behind it. Her poodles rolled around on
the bed.

"Someday all this will be yours." Georgia's voice was
muffled. There was a powder puff from Lanvin obscur-
ing her face. One of the poodles barked at her.

I assumed there was a hidden treasure in this bedroom.
Gold coins. Big diamonds. Thrones. English titles. It
seemed it could happen here.

I was the boy. She wanted this boy, never a daughter,
a thought she repeated to my mother in a shiver of
disgust whenever she could. For Georgia, I was the one
destined. I was the music box with the understood tune,
the prayer, the becoming.

Leo was a whispered word my first five years. I assumed my grandfather was my father and I worshipped
him. He was an elegant man, perfectly dressed for his
thirty years of convalescence and infirmity. He never
complained. He let my grandmother run the house, their
business, their lives.

When I heard the name Leo, I turned my head to
see my mother quickly glance in my direction, then

motion my grandmother to follow her into another room.

I snuck by, listening at a hall door.

"Goddamn that son of a bitch, you hear me?" My mother's voice. High and nasty.

"Hush, Violet. L.P. will hear you. Leo won't try. He never paid you child support. Not a Chinaman's chance." My grandmother's voice. Clenched teeth.

"Suddenly he has a new wife and now he wants to see his son? He doesn't even know L.P.'s birthday. That bastard is a big phony. A big fucking fake bastard."

"Violet!" Georgia's voice registered shock.

"What, Mother? What *now*?" I could tell my mother was angry. Her voice had become pinched and acidic, a tone that signaled a fight between Georgia and her. I knew my mother would walk out. Violet would drive, alone, into the desert. She would get lost, cry alone in my grandmother's baby blue 1959 Cadillac Fleetwood, and slowly retrace her steps on just poured, fresh tar roads that dipped and ran straight for hours, and days. It was as much of a ritual as Georgia sitting in her kitchen, taunting Betty, wrapping gold snakes around her and forming her day by consensus and bile.

As I grew older I wondered if Mother saw things in the desert, significant wonders which I took for granted but I realized not everyone could see. The way certain rocks have faces, and how these faces change with the sun's passage, sometimes old and wizened, others like clowns, dogs, or children.

I wondered if she saw clouds as spirits. The Indian women had explained this to me. They showed me by the tilt of their hands how clouds are warriors; that no cloud ever extinguishes itself, but rebuilds over the sea, to come back on land for the fight. The wind is their horse. And they are fated to only fight one another. Until it has become an art.

I was taught to hate my mother. My mother showed me how to hate my grandmother. But both women completely despised my father. Leo's name brought panic, retribution, sins with a taste.

I was also aware Violet and Georgia had secrets I would never know. They passed them on, my grandfather oblivious, by signal and breath. As a girl I thought I would be privy. As a boy I wound up completely shut out. This was a private hatred, the hysteria of a womb's mistake, and one Violet and Georgia dragged behind them like a feather boa.

I heard a vicious whisper, then a moan. Then silence. I backed away. It was too quiet behind the door.

"He's not listening, is he?" My mother sounded worried. I heard my grandmother click her tongue.

Violet opened the door. When she saw me, her face fell. The veins in her neck went slack. Beyond her my grandmother's bedroom felt like iron. I could see my grandmother's bare feet in silk hose; she always took her shoes off in her room, particularly when she was ready to have a fight with her daughter. Get comfortable. Then attack.

Violet quickly pulled on my arm, looking to see if my grandfather was watching. He was asleep in his chair, the newspaper folded over his lap, his mouth open.

I resisted. Whatever was in that room, behind a locked

door, was the enemy, and I knew this enemy was not solid. It was not like my spirits in the desert. This was something that bumped through rooms and caused pain, and it could change things. Inside I saw Georgia sitting on her king-sized bed, a satin comforter pummeled under her. Her legs were crossed like someone ready for spectator sport.

My grandmother spoke first.

"Your mother has something to tell you, L.P." She paused, trying to see if I would comprehend the seriousness of the situation, then continued.

"Something she should have told you a long time ago." She touched her chignon and gave my mother a withering, condescending stare.

"Oh, shut up, Mother." Violet walked back and forth behind me. "He's only five. He wouldn't have understood."

I could hear the rustle of my mother's bright yellow and turquoise silk sundress, a gift from my grandmother.

"L.P. could read and write when he was three. You were barely potty trained." My grandmother said this so quickly, and with such assurance, my mother stood in back of me, numb. Georgia then became flushed, and touched her neck. She spoke to me in another tone I recognized; her let's-get-down-to-business tone. It was unnaturally slow, measured, and crude.

"See, your mother made a big mistake five years ago. The only good thing to come out of it was you." I shivered. The air-conditioning made the air weep. I was wearing shorts and my knees were freezing. Georgia looked at my mother, then spoke.

"Now she's paying for it."

Mother swallowed and tried to breathe normally. She was angry. She touched her hand to her hair, then let it drop.

My mother had always said she would leave my grandmother as soon as she could afford it. As soon as she finished college. My grandmother paid for her tuition, noticed that my mother's grades were never more than average, and said little, except Violet better marry rich next time. No more shacking up with men without money.

I kept my concentration on Georgia's perfume bottles. I was afraid, if I looked at these women, they would suck me in and change my life forever. I did not know then, they had this power and always would. It was their own personal spotlight. And they only used it on each other.

Mama touched my shoulder and I flinched. She bent down in back of me and straightened my hair with her nails. They were painted hot pink; I could see they were bitten.

"L.P., you have a daddy. I kept him away from you because he isn't a nice man. He's a liar and he hits people. You don't want to see someone like that, do you?"

"I have a daddy. He's in the den," I reasoned.

My grandmother smiled. "That's right, honey."

Mama continued. Georgia motioned for me to come to her. Violet held me back. She was furious Georgia would do this, as she hadn't finished.

"See, babydoll," Violet cooed, "your real daddy's name is Leo. He wants to see you. Just for a day."

"I don't want to!" I cried. I knew I was scoring points. My grandmother smiled and straightened her shoulders. My mother wasn't finished.

"But you have to, sweetheart." Violet's eyes weren't sad. They were frightened.

My grandmother stood up and began to pace.

"Leo will steal him. Right from under your feet," my grandmother whispered sharply.

My mother stood above me, shaking her head, her eyes distinctly telling Georgia to slow down. My grandmother ignored her. Her voice got even lower. The whisper became evil.

"How would you like to never see your mama again?"

I began to cry.

"Jesus, Mother, not now!" My grandmother kept motioning for me to come to her. The bracelets on her wrists shook.

I turned and looked up at my mother. She patted my eyes with her handkerchief, and turned to Georgia.

"Now you've really done it. Jesus."

My grandmother watched me, then my mother, and spoke calmly.

"Don't you see? The child is far too upset to be taken anywhere. Leo can come back next year. When L.P.'s a little older."

"You terrified him," my mother countered, "you made him cry on purpose.

"Regardless, Violet, he cried."

There was a silence. Both women became one in my thoughts. I found it difficult to pry their faces from one that was congealed, touched by fire, and now cold.

My grandmother continued.

"You want him to see Leo? Go. Be stupid."

Georgia had a standard trick she used on my mother. She narrowed her eyes, asked questions that required only the most obvious of answers. Questions for morons. Any answer Violet gave made her look like an idiot. They were cruel, expert traps. What surprised me was that my mother was always caught.

Then Georgia said something I had never thought of. She spoke to my mother in such condescending rhythms my eyes grew wide, suddenly dry.

"Besides, Violet, your son's intelligent enough to know he wouldn't miss you *that* much. No one would."

My mother began to sob. Georgia straightened her skirt, and continued.

"Violet, if someone shot you in the head they'd hear an echo."

My mother burst into an animated lurch.

"You just don't get it, do you? He's got a court order!" Violet screamed.

"So what?" my grandmother replied.

Mother turned away, toward the sheer curtains, and pretended she was hurt.

"Listen, Violet, he'll never get L.P. If it's my last breath, L.P. gets it, you hear? I can buy and sell trash like Leo. I've eaten bigger for breakfast, honey, and you know that, little girl."

The two women sensed there was nothing more to

be said. That their damages would be medicated and perfumed, squeezed into another dress. They walked right by me, absorbed in a new thought.

I remember there is a silver you see only in women's bedrooms. Reflecting its own, manufactured colors, it is cool in summer and warm in winter. This same silver makes a diamond shine when light catches it; not rainbow colors like the reflection of crystals, but actual silver, sometimes terrifyingly cold. This silver muffles tears, telephone calls spoken in a whisper, mirrors and fate and women's faces. It is entirely female, emotionless, and it gives nothing away. I saw my two silver women in their silver bedroom, air-conditioned and dizzy with views, and I tried to see if my skin was silver, too. Or if my wet cheeks shined like diamonds, but when I looked, I saw only the hems of skirts rustling by me.

Leo did have to wait another year. Georgia saw to it. I met my father when I was six. He was a nice man, short and muscular, with a face like an apple that was still green. His voice was low and gruff. He told me he was thirty-one years old and very successful.

"Say, Lindsay, would you like to come to Minnesota next year? Maybe in the summer. You could meet your new stepmother. She's very pretty."

"What's a stepmother?" I asked. If they were like the one in *Snow White*, then they had green faces and wore black robes.

"It's my second wife, Lindsay. My first wife was . . . your mother." He said "your mother" with a distaste in his mouth. He tried to make it funny, and pretended to spit, like he swallowed watermelon seeds. Suddenly I realized I was laughing at my mother, and stopped. This man was not to be trusted. He could control my reactions.

"Her name is Stephanie and she would love to meet you."

I said nothing and stared out the window. It was a Phoenix August that kills. Leo was not used to the heat. He took his sport coat off and opened the top buttons of his shirt. His nipples protruded through thin cotton, as well as masses of curly hair. Driving me down Central Avenue in his orange, rented Chrysler, Leo glanced over and smiled at me, nodding his head. His shirt was short sleeved and I could see pimples on his arms. And more black hair. He had brown eyes like mine, only his were small, and he wore glasses. I didn't think he was handsome as George Peppard. My mother explained to me that Leo had one thing going for him. His smile and something else that she wouldn't discuss. Other than that, she said, he was a worthless human being.

I had nothing to talk to him about. I counted the date palms, the olive trees on each new block, as I did every morning, and I felt comfortable.

"Lindsay, you and I are going to have a man-to-man lunch. Would you like that?" I nodded my head at this strange man, with a distinct accent, who claimed to be my father. I reasoned I didn't look anything like him. He thought I did, and went into an expression of joy when he saw me, snapping pictures. Leo said I looked just like him. I was his image. I turned and saw my mother staring at us through the glass walls of the lobby.

She wore large, round sunglasses with white frames. She turned her back on Leo when he tried to wave to her.

His car had a plastic dog with fake fur and a bouncing head in the rearview mirror. The dog talked. I secretly knew all objects in the desert talked. But it was in a different language. I heard the dog say who is daddy? He doesn't know how to smell the wind like you, L.P. He doesn't see the Indian women when he drives past them, and they shake their heads.

My father was uncomfortable. He began to sing a humorous Czech song. I had no idea what he was singing about. He bulged his eyes for effect and banged his hands on the dashboard and steering wheel as we drove, launching into two choruses, then abruptly stopped, and looked at me.

"You know what I just sang?" He had full, chapped lips.

I shook my head "no."

"Your great-grandfather was a songwriter in Prague. This is his song. It's very funny. It's about women who eat men. They kill men and then eat them. Very funny stuff."

I folded my hands into the freon massage of my daddy's cigarettes. I thought of Betty. If she was talking about my father with my mother. I knew she wanted to see what he looked like, and stood further back, near my mother, in the lobby when he picked me up.

Leo told me about his new watch, which was made in Japan. He said everything good now comes out of Japan, and asked me if I would like to try it on. I said no.

At lunch Leo chewed with his mouth open and told me about mosquitoes in Minnesota. About cold lakes.

"So cold even in the summer you can only swim for a minute or two," Leo announced.

"Is it snow water?" I asked. I had never seen snow.

"Sure. You mean you never played in snow, L.P.?" He frowned, cut a big piece of his T-bone steak and shoved it into his mouth. Then smiled.

I pretended I was a princess and he was a king. Maybe in Italy, because I learned that's where hairy people came from. My mother was queen and we were sitting in ancient Rome.

She explained to me how you fall in love and sometimes you don't realize you have fallen in love with someone who eats with their mouth open.

"You're not listening, L.P." My father's voice cut through.

"Sure I am." I batted my eyelashes. This showed I was paying attention. My father watched me bat my eyelashes and his face became foreign.

"You're not listening at all. They even did *that* to you."

"What?" I asked.

Silence.

Like my grandmother's bedroom, silver, liquid heat gathered itself in puddles on the sidewalks outside, charged with a cruelty that only fate can extinguish. I never saw my father again, after our lunch. I never met Stephanie, and I never saw Minnesota.

He took me into the men's room after lunch to pee, and when I stood next to him, I saw his penis, and screamed. I ran out and into the ladies' room, locking myself in a stall, until he had to come and get me. It was then he seemed to know something about me that I didn't, and I realized, by the time I was ten, that I wouldn't be seeing him again.

That day, somewhere in the desert, bonfires were burning garbage. Old people were taking their medication and lying by still, chlorinated pools, with dying wasps swimming in circles. Gladiolas were being cut in hothouses and the dusk-stained, lavender mountains steamed. Somewhere far from my blue cage that formed a sky, Betty was in front of an electric fan, saying her prayers, and I was in them.

five

THERE WERE WOMEN meant to close their eyes for good. I could feel it in Chinese silk. How light has its own emotion. It was a blind stitch of yin and yang. Of Shanghai factories, scarred palms and fingers with clawed thimbles. In my ten-year-old head, I could see cities like Shanghai: rickshawed and gloved for lice, its sky a moonstone, opalescent as fish from the China Sea, crowding narrow streets. Women peered from carved doors and there was no glass. Marlene Dietrich was passing by, in black coque feathers, her perfume a litany of railroads and steam. She was my best friend. She said, "This is China, L.P. Take it and eat it alive, like squid served raw, still sliding a plate of seaweed and flowers. Here you are exotic. No one will hide you. People will want to know who you are."

Violet collected anything Chinese. She loved blind stitch silks, stretched over gilt screens and ancient pillows. On these fabrics, dragons and waves were sewn, thread by thread, onto black silk that shined like fresh paint. She explained the complexities. How certain colors meant different strata of life. Yellow was imperial; blue the merchant class. She told me they were outlawed because the women who made them developed diseases of the back and eventually went blind.

This, I learned, was the luxury of pain. I discovered the most exquisite things held death and decay in their concept, and it was thrilling to touch the pillows, collect the porcelain gods and goddesses who ruled with such spite.

Every Saturday Violet took me to oriental shops and junk stores. I was dismal at developing friends, but I could talk for hours with the owners of these stores. This was my real world. I understood rosewood chairs with busted seats, warped wood floors, black lacquer bowls with goldfish twisting in cheap reds and hints of pasted glitter. In these shops of round doors and Chinese letters, I opened scrolls with men high in gnarled clouds. I bounced, and posed to an invisible camera, on opium beds with cracked legs. I looked for secret treasures behind jade and ivory screens. I was questionless, alert, happy here, in an air of incense and jasmine soap.

In 1968, Phoenix was mad for anything Chinese. Restaurants that served Mexican food had giant Buddhas by the front door, and I rubbed their bellies with a fanaticism. Women wore Susie Wong dresses with tight seams and slits up to the hip. But if a Chinese couple were to approach you, you would treat them like anyone who wasn't white. You smiled and ignored them. I saw Violet do this.

"Mama, they wanted to know directions," I accused her, looking at her, furious and embarrassed. "Why didn't you help them?"

"They built the railroads. They'll find their way," she snapped at me. I was shocked.

We were in the same store where Betty bought her dolls. It was called the Phoenix Bazaar, and I loved the way the word bazaar rolled off my tongue. I used it constantly, substituting it for bizarre.

I knew my grandmother was somehow watching us from the ninth floor. I fantasized my schoolmates were talking about me to their parents while they watched football games on Saturday and they were laughing. I was glad to be in this dark, Chinese coin of a junk shop, in colors I understood, like amethyst, persimmon, and ebony. Violet told me I was a born collector, that I could touch something and know if it was old. She had a problem with understanding antiques.

Our third-floor flat was littered with sixties, space-age furniture, mixed with Western barroom paintings of Indians and ducks as appointments meant to impress. Chinese lanterns and Goddesses of Mercy in white plastic. Violet swore they were ivory.

"I don't see anything here, L.P. How about you?" Violet yelled listlessly across the room. We were the type of customers who never stopped talking, always to each other and from opposite ends of the store. The woman behind the counter was gray and palsied and she hated us. We came in every Saturday. We never bought.

I shouted, "No." I saw a puppet from India that caught my attention, but it didn't have a head.

"Thank you very much." Violet said this very precisely, with an icy cheeriness. The old woman behind the counter never looked up from her copy of *McCall's*, which she grabbed when we walked in. This was Violet's "you've disappointed us" voice. Soon we were in the car.

She had been in a haze all morning. I knew something was wrong. It was two days before I would spend the summer with Betty, and she hadn't told me yet.

"I want to drive somewhere." My mother's eyes were following freeway signs, and I became frightened. Lately, though not frequently, she had begun to take me with her on her trips into the desert. One day we were almost at the Mexican border. Another day, in the middle of September, right before I was to go to school, we were speeding on Highway 80 to San Diego. My mother screamed for an hour, crying then screaming again, about her mother, how she was persecuted. She told me my grandmother wanted her out of the picture, that she wanted to raise me as her own son. I was almost ten. I had heard this before. I no longer cried with her.

It was that day, on Highway 80, I saw my mother liked to escape into a different air, until she was lost, and had to find her way back, often relying on strangers, and she became calm after. I realized Violet was looking for friendships that lasted only a minute or two, but were necessary and immediate. This restored her faith. It was a medicine.

We passed towns strung like clay beads. Their names were affirmations of a history we were not compatible with. Aztec. Dateland. Mohawk. For me their names were chants. After my mother stopped screaming we were at the California border. I was terrified, wondering how we had got there so fast. Even Violet was shaken. She seemed to me a bug bouncing, aiming for a window, and that was any place but Arizona. The window was closed. The border, steel tight and locked.

It would take us four hours to drive back. Mother stopped and made a call to my grandmother. I could hear her crying in the glass telephone booth. When she put the receiver down, I saw her turn around, like a ballerina on a music box, beating the glass walls with her fists.

I prayed this would not happen again. As we turned and speeded up on the freeway ramp, the sky seemed everywhere. The desert ahead of us remained mute, relentless, and dry brown as a liver spot on a truck driver's hands. I concluded Phoenix was a liver spot. Something the sun kept trying to bleach out, and every morning it came back again.

It felt like my grandmother's silver bedroom. I surmised it held a new change in my life, perhaps one I wouldn't like, and I wasn't old enough to stop it. At that moment I learned all lines bend to touch the sky; colors are wealth and the exquisite is never lost. Like ivory chrysanthemums falling on yellow shantung, where women kept stitching tiny, tingling metal beads until their blindness sang, my mother would get lost, and I, like the Chinese who hammered in those railroad tracks, would remember how to find our way home.

DONALD
RAWLEY

{ *six* }

ON THIS PARTICULAR trip, Violet didn't waste any time.
Fifteen minutes out of Phoenix, on the southern highway to Tucson, she began to cry.

Today was hotter than normal: almost a hundred and
seven. The air conditioner could only blow hot air, so
we rolled down the windows. My mother was wearing
a peach silk dress and bright yellow plastic jewelry, and
her dark, almost black, hair came undone in the hot
wind of the road.

"Why are you crying, Mama? What's wrong?" My
voice belied my disinterest. Violet couldn't sway me
with theatrics and her own pretty terrors.

"L.P. So much has happened. I'm not sad or anything.
Actually, I'm pretty happy. But tired." She blew her
nose, one hand on the steering wheel. The car veered

into the opposite lane, but we didn't see any cars heading for us. At least not this afternoon.

I could see her hands were beginning to tremble. She had pried off her gold high-heeled sandals and was driving with bare feet whose toenails, I noted, were the same candy pink as her fingernails.

"Open me a Coke," Violet said. I got out a bottle from a tiny ice chest we kept in the backseat, and took a bottle opener in the shape of a naked woman with rubies on her nipples, opened the Coke and handed it to Violet.

We were headed for a storm, I could see it when I turned around, looking west. Blackened, rubbed clouds were rumbling in from California.

It was moth season, for they always seemed to come in June, when light is at its highest. I saw moths with wings the size of fists, attaching themselves to the saguaros and mesquite trees in a blind, scalded clutch. Passing by them on the road to Tucson, their gray wings crowded the landscape.

We drove past cracked mud shacks built by Zuni Indians with outdoor showers and junkyard sinks, abandoned, bleached, skeletal. I wondered when they were asked to leave. Who said to leave. There were still bonfires, unlit; mesquite wood and sagebrush piled into a floss of twigs and rattlesnakes.

I felt like I was on a train. I was passive, my face pressed nonchalantly against the window. I felt like it was night, that Violet and I weren't related, and I was grown up. I was handsome, or beautiful, rich, famous, mysterious. From my polished wood-and-velvet compartment I could see houses, lit up, disappearing behind me as the train ricocheted forward. Like the cement and adobe Zuni shacks, these houses glowed.

In my train compartment I thought, everyone is waiting for some kind of escape. Violet called it the next step out. She was talking to me, but I couldn't hear her.

I told myself a heart is a lit house, perched against a horizon and seen from a fast, comfortable train. We pass it; we know instinctively when we are gone the light will be turned off, by a stranger. For that moment, riding dissonant rails, we see this house. We see a heart beating. A light.

In the comfort of disappointment, this house will descend into the geography of night. We know someone was living inside. And the only way we can see it again is to take the same journey every night, on the same train. I wondered if married couples had to get on the same train every night. Just to make sure that house wasn't torn down.

My mother's voice brought me back.

"I'm doing this for you, L.P. So you have a nice place to live." I realized I had almost fallen asleep, and that I'd better keep my eyes on where we were going, if we were ever going to get back. So far we still had a lot of time before Tucson. My mother was licking her lips, watching for exit signs, wooden road signs that said you'd be a fool to enter. Those she chose with a morbid regularity.

"Listen, L.P. You need a father figure." Violet's voice was direct, sudden.

"What?" I turned my face directly at hers.

"I've got two fathers right now," I replied.

"You aren't masculine enough, L.P. Do you understand what I am saying?" Her eyes refused to look at
me. She pretended to concentrate on the road. Her
voice became singsong again. A pinched doll.

The hurt came at me and I could say nothing. I was
determined not to let her see me react.

"That's why I've decided to marry Bob. He'll be a
good dad to you. Besides," she sighed, thinking to herself, "I'm pretty sure I love him."

I reeled. We drove in silence, perhaps an hour. I was
furious. She was only pretty sure? What about me? Was
she pretty sure she loved me? I then began to see that
my mother only went through life half decided. Finally,
I collected myself and spoke.

"We better head home, Mama. There's a storm behind us."

"Oh, L.P. We're going to be so happy." I could see
she was not reasonable. In her head she had on a wedding dress, nothing large, but one that has a matching
hat and the keys to a new house. A new life, away from
Georgia, and I was being told it was because of me.
Even then, I knew it had nothing to do with me.

Violet had tired of being my mother. She wanted a
little fun. With a man. Bob was extremely dull. He
rubbed my head one day, like *Leave It to Beaver,* and
said something lame, and I ran out of the room. Violet
was laughing, drinking margaritas with salt on the rim
of the glass. They were listening to Glen Campbell. It
was sickening.

"I thought you'd be happy for me, L.P." Violet began to pout.

"No. It's not that way, Mama. If you turn the car around, we'll go back now." My heart began to beat rapidly. The storm kept inching its way over us.

"I suppose you're right." Violet stopped the car and pulled over to the side of the highway.

"Boys are supposed to have fathers, honey. Not old men, or men who aren't there, but a real man, someone to be buddies with. Right?" Violet pleaded, her voice suddenly soft.

"Yes, Mother," I countered. I copied her voice when she was pissed off at Georgia.

"Don't mimic me." Violet frowned. "Let's finish this off. We're getting married the day after tomorrow, L.P. In San Diego." She spoke evenly.

I loved San Diego.

"Mama, are we driving? Like today?" My mind was full of expeditions. Hunts for seashells in La Jolla. The Pacific Beach amusement park, with the huge roller coaster that swayed every time the car went down the first hill. I loved listening to the rush of the roller coaster, hard waves breaking the beach, rock and roll on the upside down Ferris Wheel platform, all at once.

"L.P., you're not going. You're staying the summer with Betty and her husband Frank."

My voice broke. "Why?"

"Because I need a break, dear. We have to go on a honeymoon. Spend a little time together. You're getting big. You know."

Mother looked quite beautiful in the electric half light

of the storm, the hot wind making her dark hair float around her.

I knew I could do nothing but agree. Violet seemed childlike, lost. She reached down into her purse and brought out a pink lipstick, applying it in the rearview mirror, then turned and looked at me.

"What do you say we take one more road?"

"It's going to storm." I was tired. I wanted to go to sleep.

Violet's eyes sparkled and flashed. She was trying to be fun. Glamorous. Dramatic. It didn't work.

"C'mon, L.P. You can always get us home. No one has a sense of direction like you do. Beside, do you realize, this is the last time I can go and get lost?" She giggled.

Everything spoken was so direct and simple, without mention of my grandparents, or any other high drama. I was unnerved, but I was also terrified of my mother when she got this way.

Violet started the car up and soon we were on a side road. My hands tightly clutched the seat. Soon I would have to tell her to turn back. Our conversation suddenly seemed forgotten, and Violet was singing along with the radio, to the Supremes and "I Hear a Symphony." Then she turned the radio down and pointed toward a flat, radiant mesa.

"Something's shining, L.P. See it?" Violet strained her head over the steering wheel to try to decipher the shimmering image a mile beyond us, then sat back and turned up the radio.

"No," I said to her.

I couldn't tell her it was a desert star that crawls on the ground during the day, then snaps into a fixed corner at night, to help people find their way. She wouldn't have believed me. I knew this was a fact, having been told by the Indian women. I couldn't tell her all stars get their light from the sun and give it back at night; that they move past us on deserts and oceans, or that they know how to fly and sit, very content, in the night sky, because that was their job. I realized my mother would never see these things, and I began to think my grandmother might be right about her.

seven

THE BAPTIST OUR Savior in the Lord Church was a bright turquoise, the kind that throbs in sunlight. I wondered if someone had mixed electricity in its paint. It didn't seem at all like a church. Instead of a steeple or a bell tower, there was a Japanese pagoda on the roof. And plaster statues from Nogales of Foo dogs and lions with teeth bared, one paw outstretched. I couldn't see why anyone would want to put plaster statues on a church roof, but I liked the effect.

As we pulled into the parking lot, Frank spoke quietly. Betty had nodded off under her hat in the front seat, and his voice became confiding, for just us men. Heat muffled his words. I paid attention.

"A rich lady built this right after World War Two, L.P. She went crazy not soon after she moved in. See?

It was a house once." Frank pulled our car into a dirt lot. It seemed like a long walk to me, and I couldn't understand why we parked so far away.

Frank wiped his forehead with a lace hanky of Betty's and continued.

"She wanted it fancy. When she died, no one knew what to do with it, except us Baptists." Frank grinned at me.

I smiled back. I knew he was trying to be nice to me, and I felt I was a bother to Betty and him. Mama had told me I must be very nice. She also told me Betty and Frank were being paid to take care of me. I wondered exactly how much.

Frank nudged Betty and she woke up immediately. He gave me a look that said, "Be nice, L.P., you know how Betty gets."

"Where's the boy?" she muttered. "Is the boy here? We can't lose him. We just can't. He's all we got right now." Her eyes became desperate and pink. She paused to assess where she was, then turned back to Frank.

"I was dreaming. Frank, a dream God gives when he wants you to know something, but he tells you in riddles. L.P. was missing and it was my fault. I know that." Betty turned and saw me, then began to sob. I thought she was being very dramatic. I was thrilled to be the center of attention, and that I was in an actual dream.

"Thank you, Jesus." She reached over and touched my shoulder.

"Honestly, woman." Frank scowled.

Betty continued smiling and sobbing at me. I didn't

know what to do. Then I remembered something. I spoke quietly.

"I'm here, Betty. We're going to church. Then we're going bowling," I offered. I learned very young I had to repeat things to the people I knew because they never listened to me.

"You're a little angel, L.P. That's what the dream said to me, honey. God knows these things." Betty paused and dug in her bag for the appropriate lipstick.

"Today I'm going to sing." Her eyes were bloodshot and there was a pealing symmetry in her voice. I guessed she was still pretty drunk.

"The hell you are, woman." Frank didn't wait for a reply. He groaned and got out of the car, slamming the door behind him. Betty didn't do anything. She just put her lipstick on in two exact strokes, fluffing up her hat, and turned to me.

"I can sing better than any of those fat old women, L.P. They don't like me to sing in their church because they're all jealous of who I was. That's the God's truth, boy. A lot of those people still listen to my records." Betty opened her door, then turned to me again.

"Now what does a gentleman do?" She waited.

I immediately bolted from the car and opened her car door. Frank stood watching Betty and me. I didn't know if he was amused or angry.

Betty gripped my arm tight and whispered in my ear. I could smell the bile of her margaritas, the White Witch perfume, the odor of fresh mothballs and scented tissue paper from Diamond's Department Store.

"See, what I did colored women don't do, L.P. I

made something of myself." She pushed her right foot back into her high heel.

"Most colored women just lay back and pop out kids. Not me. I was famous, L.P. Remember that." Betty straightened up and looked ahead, toward the church, past Frank and the dust of arriving cars. Frank motioned for me to let him escort her, and I let go. Betty stumbled. I heard a laugh and saw Marcelline getting out of her white Cadillac. Grover was behind her. When he saw me, he waved, and I waved back.

"Betty gone Mexican on us, Frank?" Marcelline continued to laugh. Frank shook his head like it was some big joke.

"Yeh, yeh, she feelin' no pain." Betty tried to break away from his grip, but couldn't. I heard her hoarse whisper.

"You gonna tell these women I had some cocktails? You listen to me, nigger, I am no joke. You tell them that. Betty is no joke."

I gasped. It was the first time I had heard Betty say "nigger." As we walked to church I saw why we had to park so far away. Frank was right about the church being fancy. It had an acre of dusty gardens and shrines, under rows of date palms and crows. I began to run, toward this squandered, ancient wonder, leaving Frank and Betty to the long walk and adult miseries.

I came to this little red Chinese bridge, perched over a stagnant pond. There was a Chinese gazebo next to it, also red, cracked, and bloody with age. Statues peeked out from overgrown cacti and yellowed succulents. I saw the Virgin Mary and a lifesized Jesus with open arms, his face and hands painted black, an extended, thumping heart carved into his chest like a sore, painted the same red as the bridge and gazebo. Beyond him were Mexican plaster cobras sitting on ornamental rocks, sprayed gold and silver. I saw a sign near this pond and realized it was a wishing well. I threw a dime into it and made a wish. Something fast, uttered without feeling on my tongue, that wouldn't be too important if it didn't come true.

My dime fell quickly into a green bilge. There were plastic water lilies with melted votive candles in their centers, stuck on top of the thick water. I looked for the coin. Suddenly I wanted to set everything right: put new candles in these water lilies, and have all of them floating in a clear, chlorinated lagoon.

Instead of half-dead, angry cacti, there would be lush trees with flowers and vines. Johnny Weissmuller would be swimming naked in the pond and I would be naked with him, but much prettier than Jane. Then we would kiss in the lagoon and climb onto rocks and do adult things.

I was enchanted. Here I could be Ursula Andress, She Who Must Be Obeyed, and recite prayers to angry volcanoes. The statues were alive, I just knew it. And Jesus approved. He was keeping His eye on me this Sunday in June.

I believed that all ugliness could be repaired, that shabbiness was a beauty waiting for me to touch and transform. I found magic in the chipped and cracked, the torn and forgotten. My eyes saw only what could be, and I understood the charm of possibility.

Behind me I heard Betty and Frank arguing in low voices about me. Then Marcelline's light chatter. Above me date palms, untrimmed and musky, sported beards and murmured fictions. Their green fronds made music in the early summer wind, and I stood very still, trying to count palms, water lilies, cobras, and other statues I assumed hid the graves of very holy black people. In front of me there was music, coming from a turquoise church with carved doors. This was better than miniature golf.

"Bet you there are fish in the pond?" It was Grover's voice. He was behind me, getting ready to drop a large piece of quartz into the water.

"Where did you find that?" I asked. The quartz was rosy, and it sparkled.

"Right over there. Lots of it. Mother says it's expensive. But I want to drop one and kill a fish like the Eskimos do." He dropped his chunk of quartz and bent down, peering over curtained, dismal water.

"There aren't any fish in there," I said flatly. Grover looked at me and smiled. He wanted to be my friend. I liked him, but I thought dropping a pretty rock into a smelly pond was not particularly bright.

"I know there are fish. There have to be. Where there's water, there's fish," he screamed.

"All I see are some cigarette butts," I said. I didn't want him to get upset or loud, because I knew Marcelline and Betty would come over. I was right. I could hear Betty's voice.

"L.P. Come back here. You, too, Grover. There's church to do. You mind the snakes and scorpions out there! Come on now!" We both turned and saw the adults standing in front of the ornate church doors. Betty leaned against Frank and looked very regal, Marcelline standing slightly behind her. Betty was trying to be coherent. She looked to me like she was trying to wipe something off.

Grover and I followed the adults into the church. I was angry. All I wanted was to stay in that ruined garden for the rest of my life. I would repaint the bridge and gazebo, build a palace, become famous and then charge admission. It made perfect sense. And I knew it was better than ever going home.

Upon entering, I smelled lemon oil and stock field lilies, a stench I had never encountered. Frank breathed in deep and touched my hand.

"We donate them from the mortuary. The ones with a day or two left. They stink up the room the best." He seemed quite proud of himself.

"Smells like a poor funeral to me," Betty muttered, looking for her pew. There were four pews in back and Betty slid into one like she was a movie star who didn't want to be noticed. The rest of the room had folding chairs set in neat rows, all full. There was a sea of hats, of paper flowers and yellow and white dresses.

The church's stained glass windows weren't religious, but geometric patterns of colored glass. The floors shined. They were dark wood and the cleanest, most perfect thing about this room. The pulpit was huge, carved with Indonesian dancers, that looked like it had originally been a chest. I loved Indonesian dancers with hand bells and pointed gold hats. I read about them in school and thought they were very elegant.

In front of us, Grover turned and winked at me. I saw Samuel and waved, but he didn't see me. I wondered if he would remember me. I hadn't seen him for many months. His head was bowed down, and his glasses looked like they would slip off. His mother seemed very angry with him, pushing his back straight, throwing a Bible on his lap like it was a bone. I didn't like Samuel's mother. She was wiry and wore horn-rimmed glasses with rhinestones and her skin was dirty brown with white spots on her neck. She never seemed happy, and always was pushing and slapping Samuel, who was gentle and sweet.

I thought about how I could use the pulpit as a tiny house. Or a secret hiding place for important things. Behind the pulpit was a white neon cross, turned on for Sunday services. It was mesmerizing, brighter than anything I had seen. I paced myself as I stared at it, treating it like I would the desert sun. I stared directly into its white burn, counted to ten, then closed my eyes to see the white spots.

There were snowflakes the color of flame, passing under my eyelids in an unconscious dance. These spots could not be controlled by me; I could manufacture them, by staring into an afternoon sun, or the white electric fuzz of a Baptist cross, but I could not hold them. They faded on their own, like flowers breaking.

I thought of what blind people must feel. If electric crosses and suns and hospital lights make dancing spots under their eyelids. If they are capable of recognizing them, if they enjoy them when they happen. If they think all light is just a white spot crawling over their eyes, up into a memory in their brain.

I opened my eyes and the spots were gone. A preacher named Denzel Epoch had ascended the podium and was clearing his voice. The room quieted down. In back of him, he turned on a record player, and I head Mahalia Jackson singing, but I couldn't make out the words. The record was scratched.

Two black people came in with afros and the room stopped. Heads turned around to see them, then shook themselves in disgust. It was a young black couple, and they were dressed in African clothes and had on dark sunglasses. I thought they looked very dangerous and glamorous. No one else did.

They passed around leaflets, but no one would take them, and two elderly women shooed them away as the service was about to start. Mr. Epoch cleared his throat one last time, turned Mahalia Jackson off and asked the congregation to rise and sing a song. I couldn't hear what song it was, but suddenly there was a roar.

And it didn't stop for an hour. People clapped their hands and sank to their knees. Betty swayed and clapped her hands, showing me how to clap mine, and I tried to mouth the words, but everyone seemed to know this one song and there weren't any choir books, like at Catholic church. A heavy woman dressed in burgundy, with flat shoes and swollen ankles, began going crazy, shaking her wrinkled arms and crying, singing and laughing at the same time as though Jesus were playing her like a marionette. I kept time with my feet.

In this whitened air, the scream of a psalm made my skin twitch. I tried to keep the blindness in, the white spots crossing over my pupils, but soon the congregation came back in a mist.

Frank couldn't sing. He mouthed words, looking uncomfortable. An elderly colored man sank to his knees, clapping, slowly advancing knee by knee, singing in a palsy toward Denzel Epoch's pulpit. Denzel didn't seem particularly concerned. An elderly black lady, probably the old man's wife, skittered up to him like a cross sparrow, pulling him up and making him walk to the back of the church.

Denzel Epoch kept clapping, sneaking looks at his watch. He was wearing a white suit, white shoes, and a white tie, and over that a purple-and-yellow satin open robe. I thought he looked like an Easter egg.

I thought of the word passionate. There was passion here. I was ready to accept a black God along with my white Gods, my movie stars, zombies, vampires, my mother and grandmother. At that moment I knew I still had enough room inside.

I realized we were singing without an organ or a record or even a piano, and the music was delicious, mounting upon itself until I thought we couldn't go any further, but we did, and I then realized in the hysteria, that I was the only white boy there. And I liked it. It made me special. I wasn't being asked why I acted like a girl, or why I was so skinny, or shy, or such a dreamer. I could keep the beat here.

As fast as it started, the roar stopped. People still stood

waiting, fanning themselves, laughing, taking sips of whiskey and iced tea and ice water from thermoses.

Betty began to sing. I jumped away from her, wondering if she was going to make a fool of herself. Frank massaged my shoulder and made me stand straight up, next to him. He didn't smile.

Her voice came out pure and low and measured. She stared up at the ceiling of the church and I saw that everyone was watching her, fanning themselves. I hoped they would be kind to her. Not make fun of her, or talk behind her back. Betty sang about climbing a golden staircase. She didn't move her arms, only craned her neck up in a simple, refined gesture. Frank smiled at her. Her eyes were white as the electric cross, as the birds on her lace covered cheeks, as the gloves she put on for church.

Three lines into her song, the roar began again, and it came with such force on her lines I sat down, exhausted. The beat got faster and men screamed along with women. Betty sat down next to me and composed herself. She took out a vial from her purse and drank the entire contents, then put it back. I could see her mouth words meant for me.

"You see, L.P., I can sing."

It was the reflection of a mute, of words spoken under an orchestra. She closed her eyes. I realized we both had seen the spots; we both wanted the reality of blindness, if only for an instant, a white that could scald shadows. A sea of white. Soft, clean, white water, white clouds and numb white skin that washes off pain. White lives. White. White.

eight

IT WAS AN hour after Baptist services had finished. The air was a Frank Sinatra orange, a glow that could draw blood with its heat. Grover and I had taken off our clip-on bow ties. I did it because I hated anything with a collar. Grover did because his neck was too fat and, during services when we had to sing, he gasped for breath between hymns.

I was in the backseat of Marcelline's Cadillac Coupe de Ville, next to four bowling ball bags laid reverently on the floor, two of them under my feet. I could feel the hardness of those marble balls with my heels. I let my heels slide up and down the bags until I got bored.

Marcelline was driving. I couldn't see Grover in the front seat because the seats were so high, with extra thick headrests in soiled white leather. The entire interior of the Cadillac seemed a soiled white, like an angel who found sex. Leather was cracking and there was a brown fuzz on its white shag carpeting. I couldn't decide if it was lint or some sort of adult dirt I didn't know about.

Marcelline called her car "The Honey Bee," and I found little brass nameplates that read "Marcelline" in curved letters. They had fallen off and were tucked in a pouch on the back of the front seats, along with an ebony Jesus, two paperback road maps, and empty airline liquor bottles. I never saw a black Jesus before, and rubbed his face with my palm. As for the liquor bottles, I tried collecting them once, from empty lots and trash at the apartment building, until Georgia found out. I assumed Marcelline liked to fly.

She had worn shocking pink to church; shocking pink gloves, satin hat, pumps, and dress. Even her pearls were pink. It made her skin seem fresh, like just cooled chocolate, and with her false eyelashes and hair ironed into a greasy flip, she looked like an entertainer. Or a whore. I thought how no white woman could get away with that much color. But on Marcelline it was tropical, glamorous. She was a hybrid. An expensive, neon tone, like salt-water fish I couldn't afford.

Grover was complaining he was hungry.

"Hush, Grover. You don't hear L.P. complaining, do you? We have to go to the train depot for a few minutes. You can show L.P. the cattle cars. Then we'll go to the Desert Bowl. They have fresh pies at the coffee shop, L.P." Marcelline turned and smiled at me in a pretty, flirty way, giving me a wink. I had never been winked at before. Her eyelashes looked heavy.

Marcelline took a turn too fast and I grabbed the open window. The smell of eucalyptus, irrigation canals, and gasoline poured into me, then quickly traveled on. In the backseat I watched, fascinated, as she maneuvered the car through a potholed road, applied lipstick, smoked a cigarette, and read directions at the same time. Grover turned and laughed at me.

"Mother can't drive." He always called Marcelline "Mother." I thought him very formal, like an English lord. Grover's eyes began to squeeze into delighted coins.

"Mother has a new boyfriend at the train station and he's going to give us free steaks from Omaha. The ones they pack in ice that are real expensive." He slid back into his seat and I heard Marcelline click her tongue; I could see her give Grover a foul, un-pretty look. At a red light she arched her neck around to me.

"It's no big deal, L.P. Do me a favor and don't tell Betty, okay?"

I nodded my head. I was too tired to say much. Marcelline continued to look at me, to see if I grasped her words. She decided to speak slowly, weighing down her voice, which was normally a shrill caw, like mockingbirds early in the morning.

"No. You tell Betty I'm saving these steaks when I get 'em for the church barbecue in July. You tell her that. They'll be in my freezer. No one will eat them."

Her reasons were unclear to me, but she seemed satisfied, and put her foot on the gas.

I still didn't understand why I should be driving with Marcelline and Grover to the Desert Bowl. I knew

Frank was angry with Betty for being drunk. I knew Marcelline was Betty's best friend. She wanted Grover to be my best friend. I wasn't so sure.

At service's end, not an hour before, Betty had told me to go with Marcelline, that she and Frank had several things they had to discuss. Betty said she would meet us at the Desert Bowl, go on, it was safe. Her voice wasn't slurred anymore, but her eyes were red.

Frank was talking with the minister, Denzel Epoch, and an old colored man named Larry. Larry was a foot shorter than Denzel and had large moles on his neck. He wore golf slacks and white buck shoes. The men were laughing in deep growls about golf and women and church. Something about a Hawaiian barbecue and hula skirts. And Jack Daniel's. Light poured through stained glass in a warm silence. I figured God as warm and silent, and He was made of colored glass. God sat around churches after everyone left and took notes.

Here there was a musk I had never encountered. These colored ladies smelled different. When they wore perfume I dreamed of green places with trees so dense they hid the sun. Where you couldn't breathe unless you pulled away branches from treetops, or hacked through walls of flowers. I liked this place, these women. It wasn't the smell of powder. It was the smell of being thrown into a lagoon; of reaching up for passion flowers and narcissus, their pollen on wet arms becoming a fragrant mud.

The church wasn't air-conditioned, and the last couples to leave, after chatting with Denzel Epoch, fanned

themselves with newspapers. Some women brought lace
fans and fans from China. Others folded them out of
church programs and they created the most air.

Betty weaved behind me, her hands on my shoulders,
and I knew I had to walk straight or she would fall
down. We glided past Frank and Larry and Denzel
Epoch. They stopped, smiled, watched Betty. Larry studied me out of his eyes, which had gray cataracts.

"The heat, oh dear, this heat!" Betty fluttered, trying
to cool herself off by taking off her bird hat and waving
it with one hand. I could see where her hair had become
creased and flat with perspiration.

Under her breath she said, "Get me the hell out of
here, L.P. Now."

I could see Frank's forehead glisten with sweat. He
gave me a dirty look. Suddenly I was frightened. When
we got to the wavering, reckless shade of a date palm
outside, I turned to Betty.

"Frank wants to kill me," I confided.

Betty slowly slid down against the palm, onto the
dead grass. Her skirt crinkled up around her hips.

"He hasn't known you long enough." She smiled at
me through these words, laying like a cat ready to clean
itself. One of the birds from her hat caught on the husk
of the palm. I took it, knowing she would not retrieve
it. I planned to give it to her later, so everything would
stay in place, and she could continue her diary of appropriate hats; when they were worn, and when they could
be retired.

"I just have to rest for a minute, honey. You go with

Marcelline. Frank and I will meet you at the bowling
alley. Go on."

I didn't realize Marcelline was right behind me when
she took my hand and walked me toward her white
Cadillac. Her rings scratched my palm and I didn't mind.
At ten I never let any woman, even my mother, hold
my hand, because you were supposed to walk alone. But
I could smell that lagoon on Marcelline's fingers and I
liked it. I liked being lost, taken away from anyone who
ever knew me.

Before I got in the car I looked at Betty. Her chin
was resting on her chest. Date palm blossoms blew down
lazily on her shoulders. She seemed broken and twisted
in front of the Baptist Our Savior in the Lord Church,
left to rot, or worse yet, come alive again in the orange
stain coloring this afternoon. Frank was walking up to
her, wiping his forehead with a white hankie. I got in
the car.

"Right here we make a left." Marcelline attempted
another screaming turn, and I was someplace new. This
was one road I had not charted. I began to see the train
signs, and cafe signs that read "The Phoenix Station,"
"The Whistle Bar," "Oleta's Train Track Club." They
had blacked-out windows with paintings of men playing
pool. Of saxophones and women in chiffon baby-doll
tops with words like "topless" and "exotic" pasted over
their breasts.

Grover noticed the signs,too, and turned back to look
at me, giggling.

"Titties!" he said, and Marcelline hit him. He recoiled, sinking into the seat, and turned on the radio. It was religious music, just like the scratched records at church. I heard Mahalia Jackson start to sing again, and smiled. I liked Mahalia Jackson. She was very dramatic, and always ended her songs with long, hurricane notes. Then bowed her head.

Suddenly I noticed black men everywhere, like boulders hiding a canyon. I noticed right away they moved faster than in the movies, and none were playing the harmonica. Growing up, I thought black men in a group became slow because they were without their women, and therefore unhappy. But here the men moved fast.

There were black men in white silk suits moving through clusters of black men hauling flanks of beef. I saw the innards were still attached, dangling and leaving a trail on the sidewalk. Sepia men in T-shirts covered with sweat and bits of flown fat, opened boxes with enormous pliers and wrenches. Black men hopped into taxis that looked like bumblebees, ones I never saw on Central Avenue. And I realized, as I looked around, I was the only white person around. I was too entranced to be frightened.

Marcelline seemed to sense what I was thinking, and as she slowed down through the crowd, she lit a cigarette and talked to me through the rearview mirror.

"You know, L.P. This is our side of the tracks. All you have to do is walk around. No one will hurt you here. Not one hundred feet away the white people have their railroad station. We never go there. And they never come here. Are you scared?"

I shook my head "no." I was speechless, beyond

happy. Now, finally, I was in China. Grover and I were going to meet the Shanghai Express.

Marcelline continued.

"Has your mother ever told you about the wrong side of the tracks?" Marcelline arched her head, looking out the window at the different men. Some waved. Some smiled. Their teeth were white as December clouds.

"For her, L.P., and probably for you as you get older, this is the wrong side. But for us it's the right side. You see?" She tossed her cigarette out the window.

"Mother . . ." Grover began to whine.

"I'm not finished," Marcelline snapped. She went on, in a slightly more subdued voice. I knew Grover and I were in for a lecture. I didn't even know Marcelline that well, but I could always tell when an adult was ready to give speeches, advice, lectures on what is right in life. The air becomes stale; they pause for effect, and then speak slowly to you, to make sure you aren't retarded. They almost never look you in the eye.

"That means, L.P., there are two sides of the track. The beef they take off these cars is just as good as what white people eat, pay big money for. We eat the same meat, L.P. You get it?"

"Sure. You're right!" I exclaimed, and Grover looked at me, sighing in relief. This meant his mother was satisfied. The last bit of Sunday piety was gone. Now we could concentrate on boyfriends, steak, bowling, and booze.

"Are we at the trains yet?" I feverishly asked.

Marcelline shook her head.

"Almost though, honey. Almost."

Through the open window steam came in and it paralyzed me. It was death, ovens and dust. Meat on hooks disappeared into buildings. Suddenly I heard the sound of cows. I could smell their hides. Their tails softly switched at flies. Many of the men we passed wore beige and orange zip-up bodysuits, some wearing face masks and plastic eyewear, like a science fiction movie, carrying ropes and blunt instruments covered in blood. I saw a conductor with a striped cap drink a bottle of Coke, then wipe his sleeve, open his fly, and turn against an adobe wall. Past him, German shepherds shaved for fleas were snapping at bits of meat thrown out of a boxcar, and I realized we were at the railroad.

Marcelline stopped the car in a dust lot next to two butterscotch colored trucks. In one of them a black man in a straw cowboy hat was asleep, his cowboy boots on the dashboard. He wore cool James Bond sunglasses and Grover told me this was Marcelline's boyfriend. Marcelline slammed the Cadillac door and walked to the truck.

She reminded me of Marilyn Monroe in *Niagara*, walking in her red dress away from the camera, only this dress was shocking pink satin, shining so hard in the sun it looked like it hurt. The way Marcelline rubbed her legs together, as she walked, made her seem to be hiding something, a briefcase of cash, or a machine gun, up that dress. I remember the heat in her dirty white Cadillac, the fact I was only half aware of where I was.

"Mother's a widow, and that's why she has a boyfriend. She says you can't live without a good man."

Grover whispered this to me, as though this was of the highest confidentiality.

"Mother wears yellow lace nighties without a bra when he stays over. I've seen her titties." He smiled broadly. "Guess what his name is?"

"What?" I asked.

"It's William. Isn't that a dumb name for a boyfriend?" Grover watched his mother smile up at the black cowboy in the truck, then nod at him gently. As he came to, we could see through the sun and train fumes Marcelline slowly reach up and lightly kiss him on the cheek, very coy, a pink stoplight next to a train.

"I hate her," Grover said simply. He opened a stick of gum and offered me one, which I took.

"Let's get out and look at the cattle," I volunteered. I was beginning to perspire in the Cadillac. We got out and ran toward the cattle cars parked next to a large warehouse. I could hear grunts and a shuffling of hooves. We heard Marcelline scream from behind us, "Five minutes!" but we were too preoccupied to care. I didn't run fast, because Grover wouldn't be able to keep up. His stomach was too big, and I knew he couldn't always see his feet.

"L.P., why do you always run like a girl?" Grover asked, nicely, when we came up to an open, half-caged door to a cattle car. He was panting.

"I don't know. Maybe if you were skinny you'd run like me, too." I wasn't trying to be mean. I didn't really care at that moment. Grover thought about this briefly.

"You know, you're probably right." I didn't realize then Grover had been taught to believe that white people were right all the time. You either agreed or you didn't. If you didn't, there were other towns where perhaps you might be willing to agree.

I looked at him. He took off his beige coat that Marcelline had embroidered a boarding school coat of arms on, which embarrassed him, but fit his English gentleman image. The buttons of his shirt were stretched painfully. Grover was almost six inches taller than me, which didn't say much, but at the moment I though he had probably grown as much as he was going to. His lips were very large, larger than Marcelline's or Betty's, or even Frank's, and he had light brown eyes that were almost yellow. His nose was squashed in. I realized he could be easily hurt, just like me; his face was something things bounced off. Where I had developed a hard, pretty little face, his was like rubber. They were both masks, and I knew we would grow up a lot tougher than we looked. I began to like Grover at that moment.

Suddenly, something wet flew on the back of my neck. Grover laughed. I turned and looked up at the car. A cow was staring at us, and had blown a clear liquid out of its nose on me.

"Cow snot! Cow snot!" Grover screamed with delight. The sun was so cruel we didn't stay long. He began to breathe heavily. I looked up at the cow who looked at me from the shadows of its hay-strewn coffin. There were other cows in back of it.

"Sure stinks around here, L.P. Let's go back to the car." Grover looked up at the afternoon sun.

I stood mesmerized, staring into the cow's eyes. I knew cattle were stupid. I wondered what I must look like to that cow. If it knew I was of the same breed that would eventually kill it, eat it. If it cared at all.

"They're all going to die," I whispered.

"So? I like steak. And hamburgers. Let's have a cheeseburger when we get to the bowling alley. C'mon." Grover began to walk back. I followed him, stepping gingerly over the train tracks.

"I thought there'd be movie stars getting out of the train. And reporters and stuff," I said, walking beside him toward the Cadillac.

"That's Hollywood and white people, L.P. Here we got cows." Grover seemed annoyed. I had spots in my eyes from the sun, and they were that cow's dulled eyes. Perhaps the cow knew it was dead, and didn't bother to tell me, or make a sign.

At the car, we saw Marcelline in an embrace behind the open trunk. William had his hands over her rear end and he rubbed each buttock with a slow, circular grip. Grover stopped and made me stop as well, signaling me to watch. We began to giggle.

Marcelline broke away. She tripped over a stone and bent down to readjust the strap on her spike heel, then stood up and faced us with a pursed, slightly smeared smile.

"Boys, look what William gave me. Just look at this trunk." Marcelline proudly displayed the contents. Inside, I saw ice that still was dry, smoking, and fifty or more red steaks. I knew when we drove the ice would become wet and begin to melt. Water would leak out of her trunk and she could be stopped by police if they thought it looked like gas. She would leave the bowling alley early, make some excuse, then put those steaks in her freezer. I promised myself I would not give her secrets away.

"Look!" Grover put his hand square on a chunk of steaming ice. I was fascinated. Suddenly Marcelline began to scream.

"Jesus, don't do that!" She tried to get Grover's hand off the ice, but it was stuck. He became frightened, staring at me, silently asking me what to do.

"You'll lose skin you little fool!" she cried. William laughed, walked slowly over and poured the contents of his beer over Grover's hand, yanking it off quickly. He looked at me, then turned to Marcelline.

"Who's the white boy?" I heard William ask. I heard Marcelline take him aside, then whispers and laughter. Grover got in the car. He was crying from embarrassment. I swung myself around, toward the cattle cars, ready for Prescott and two-step, four-corner towns. Marcelline was motioning for me to get into her white Cadillac, but she was only a momentary silhouette on the even whiter sun. I could hear the cattle. I imagined them racing past closed depots, ditchwater farms of green beans, gravel roads and vinegar air. Out of Phoenix and its two-sided tracks. Out of the earth and into the sky.

I knew they would not see the puzzles of blackened, incendiary plains, the slits of old light and sage. They wouldn't feel their flesh attached, like a child's hand to dry ice, to the hook, because their eyes would be taken away. Suddenly I knew this is how we went to heaven. In our own manure, on a rusty track, with our faces to the wall. I shuddered, wanted to speak a comfort, but there wasn't any time. The Cadillac door closed shut. Marcelline lit a cigarette and turned on the radio. Grover looked back in my direction and grinned, and I knew, no matter where I went, sooner or later, I would be able to smell the stockyards and know how the train engines start.

{ *nine* }

THE COLORED LADIES Bowling League of South Phoenix met at the Desert Bowl every second Sunday of the
month, all year long. Teams played for a yearly competi-
tion, and teams were large, comprised of over sixty
women each, revolving on a seasonal basis. There were
secretaries and presidents and treasurers who kept count
of the funds, complicated scoring and banquets. Prizes
were given at the end of each year for the winning team.
Prizes included new Cadillacs, trips to Hawaii, and mink
stoles. Socializing was kept in house. Winning teams had
more social clout. The Colored Ladies Bowling League
of South Phoenix was big time.

The Desert Bowl was in a white neighborhood, but
those Sundays were reserved for the ladies of South
Phoenix, who filled its cocktail lounge and coffee shop

and gift store, and no one had time to be segregated. The Desert Bowl made far too much money. These ladies ran the Desert Bowl on those Sundays with a precision that was breathtaking. In by two in the afternoon, after noon church, then out by eight that evening. No parking lot accidents, no drunken scenes, no men. Bowling for prizes and cash was serious business; the cocktail lounge even had its own pecking order. Who's seen at whose table. The best booths reserved for that year's winning team. Losers sat at the bar.

Grover and I were sitting in the coffee shop with Betty and Marcelline, eating cheeseburgers and cherry pie. Betty and Marcelline were on the losing team. We were waiting for our turn to play, and Betty was sobering up with iced coffee.

Marcelline kept her eyes on Grover and me, making sure the conversation didn't turn to meat. Every time we began to speak, she interrupted in her baby doll voice, telling Betty how wonderful her voice sounded in church, how exciting it was that people knew who she was.

"I still work as a maid," Betty muttered. Betty looked at me and smiled. "L.P. is the only reason I stay. Someone's got to protect him."

"What do you mean?" Marcelline toyed with the beets in her salad as Betty took another sip of her iced coffee.

Betty checked to see if I was paying attention and I was, but I pretended to listen to Grover rattle on about cheeseburgers and cows. Satisfied I was in a child's world, Betty continued in a low voice.

"What I mean, honey, is L.P. is different. You know that. And those two women are going to kill him. They don't have love in their hearts. They're barren."

"Kill him?" Marcelline stared at me vaguely.

Betty was annoyed. She fidgeted in the greased, coffee steam air of the restaurant.

"Oh, for Christ sake, Marcelline. His mother and his grandmama treat him like a poodle. A pet. They don't see the little boy."

I felt chilled. I thought I was going to cry. No one had ever voiced the thought that Violet and Georgia didn't love me. The thought seemed suffocating, like graveyard mud. I didn't blink. I continued to listen to Grover giggle and Betty whisper.

"I'm set that this child have a decent Christian summer. Do all the little things boys do. Climb trees. Get dirty. Run."

I couldn't tell Betty that I spent my time sitting in her bedroom looking at her chiffon dresses and hats, watching television and dreaming.

"Back in Hollywood I had a little boy. He was white, but he was mine. You understand?" Betty lit a Kool. Marcelline nodded her head. I looked up briefly. She didn't have a clue.

"Then he goes and disappears. I don't even know how my little baby died." Betty's voice cracked. Across the table, I could see Marcelline pat Betty's hand.

"We've been through this before, buttercup." Marcelline sounded insincere, halted, as though seeing a blemish in the mirror.

"It's not going to happen this time." Betty's voice drifted off and I knew the subject would change, filed away for another Sunday and the long ride of margaritas and heat.

"If it makes you feel any better, honey, I'm a maid too," Marcelline said, managing a smile. This was news to Betty, and she lifted her head and stared at Marcelline.

"We're all maids, Betty. That's how the book was written." Marcelline stared out into the coffee shop. Waitresses wore black-and-white uniforms and had pink plastic roses on their lapels. Our table fell silent. I could hear the *click-click* of the dessert cart wheels making its way through the room.

"My mother is a housekeeper, not a maid," Grover growled.

His eyes were fierce. I was terribly proud of him. Particularly that he was eavesdropping the same way I was, and I hadn't known. I suddenly realized he must have heard what Betty said about me.

The two women began to laugh nervously. Marcelline became pointed and fierce.

"There are certain things you aren't supposed to hear. Both of you go get your shoes." We rose. I looked at Betty for a sign. She nodded her head at me, and I could see her eyes. They were frightened. I smiled.

"I've never bowled before," I said softly. I loved Betty.

Betty grinned and patted her marcelled hair.

"Well, L.P., I'll teach you. Now you go get a pair

of shoes from the front desk. They shouldn't be loose, remember. We'll be out in a bit. Marcelline and I have to go to the ladies room and put on our slacks."

I couldn't tell Betty I was terrified of holding a bowling ball and trying to score points in front of sixty black women. I couldn't tell her I didn't want to be a boy. Or that being a boy was work, something I had to think and act out before I did it, in order to get all the moves right. I understood artifice. I had to act out the role of a boy at school to survive. It was unnatural as the flu. If I let my realities show through, my world of decayed gardens and Sophia Loren and Indian women who raised their arms to ghosts, I would be beaten.

I was always smart enough to blend. But if I wasn't hurt physically, I walked through taunts like fields of wildflowers, and the whistles of boys became the hum of planes taking me into the sky, the cadence of exotic birds at my feet. I promised myself to never let them see my emotions. I knew I would become rich and famous and come back to Phoenix from Europe or Hollywood armed with a mouthful of spit. But I wouldn't spit on them. I would let them know I forgot who they were.

Even then, at the Desert Bowl Coffee Shop and Grill, I was busy forgetting. I forgot Betty's voice in church, what she had just said to Marcelline. I decided to forget Violet and Georgia, at least for the day. I made up my mind to forget state borders and silver bedrooms and sunsets. I knew present tense was all that mattered. I was going bowling.

★ ★ ★

When our turn came, Betty stepped up to the lanes in a beige pantsuit. She didn't look so hunched or unhappy. She made hand gestures that I thought were funny and I laughed. I looked around. All the Colored Ladies Bowling League of South Phoenix were wearing slacks, their Sunday church outfits on hangers, wrapped in cellophane, and lying on plastic chairs with yellow scooped seats. No one sat down very long, and if they did, it was to light a cigarette or sip a beer.

A plain woman in purple slacks and a white T-shirt yelled out at Betty.

"Go for it, Betty honey!" Betty stood very still, pulled her knees together and swung the ball low. It plopped and gathered momentum. All the pins went down. I watched, fascinated. The idea of being able to do this was exhilarating.

"It's your turn, L.P.," Betty said to me.

I got up. Grover made a fart noise with his mouth and hands and laughed. Betty directed me over to the ball drop. I realized I was swishing as I walked, and I tried to shake my legs, then amble over with my knees not so close together.

"Take that ball, L.P. It's light." Betty gently put my hand over the ball, which looked like a blue, slick marble.

"Now, get the feel of it. That's right. Stick your fingers in like so. Correct. Now bend your elbow and hold the ball with your hand under it. No, bend your left knee. No. Your LEFT knee. Correct. Now, you saw how I did it. You do the same. Walk slow, then fast. You like to swim. Think that you are on a diving board, then you get ready to dive. Go on." Her voice was soothing. Like I was sick and needed aspirin.

I did as Betty said. I had visions the ball would not leave my fingers. That I would disappear behind the pins and the ladies would laugh. I let go of the ball and it went into the gutter. Grover made another fart noise.

I turned and looked at Betty, Marcelline, Della, and Grover. Della marked my score under the tiny desk lamp, a cigarette dangling on her lips, and shook her head. Marcelline and Betty stared at me oddly. I felt they did not know what to say to bring things back to normal. They were thinking, expressionless, their faces dark alabaster. Grover was licking a Reese's Peanut Butter Cup off his fingers. Marcelline sighed.

"Your turn, Grover," she said, ignoring her son.

Grover finished licking his candy, then stood up and went over to the balls. He looked extremely confident. He picked up a heavy black ball. Betty turned to Marcelline.

"That's professional weight," she murmured. Marcelline grunted and scowled. Grover began to mimic the way I walked up to the lane.

"Stop it right now, son." Marcelline turned to see if I noticed. I sat down, pretending to be absorbed in the score sheet. Grover took a very deep breath. Betty giggled.

"Marcelline, that kid has a set of pipes. You should put him in choir."

Then Grover scooped his fat body low and released the ball into the lane and it ran. I watched it hit every pin. Perfect score. He turned and smirked, then sat down next to me as if he hadn't done anything.

"Want some licorice?"

"You did real good," I said. "I made a fool of myself. Everybody saw me."

"No one cares, L.P. I could be a champion bowler, but soon as Mother sees me winning she steps in and takes over my moves. She can't bowl worth shit." He lowered his voice to a whisper.

" 'Sides, you're white and you're not real strong yet. Rich kids never are."

I lowered my eyes and stared at the floor. He was right. I was furious.

"I'll learn how. I swear I will."

"Ooh look. Sugar Babies." Grover completely dismissed me as he dug his fingers into his bag of candy.

I thought of how air carries seeds to rich soil. How I could be flown someplace else, carried haphazardly to a mountain or beach that no one knows. I made myself play for the entire afternoon, and I finally began to score. I watched the Colored Ladies Bowling League become tense, slap each other on the back by seven and begin the arduous process of packing, saying good-byes, organizing cocktail parties and school rides, shopping trips to Nogales. They waited patiently in line, laughing and gossiping, to return their shoes. The cellophane of their church dresses rattled and shimmered behind them like the wind, like the clouds that hung low over the Gila River and disappeared, carrying trees and pollen to wetter states where these same Colored Ladies spoke slower and green was not an unusual color. Their sons and daughters were like me. We wanted to fly in the wind, toward any casual, mistaken spot, and that's where we'd grow. No one here sensed this. Maybe they did, but kept silent.

Betty patted me on the back. Her breath wasn't stale now.

"You did just fine, L.P. By August you'll be scoring big." As we pushed open the double glass doors, the heat blew on our faces until we had to close our eyes.

"I'm proud of you." Betty rubbed her forehead. I said nothing.

Marcelline kissed me on the cheek and Grover blanched. As we got in our cars, I kept counting, keeping figures; the shoes returned, the points scored, the fear in my arms. How many times I would bowl this summer. I knew what to do. Like the rest of my life, I would adapt and hide, finding the most convenient shadow of the Desert Bowl and wait for my turn to come up, roll the ball and hope the pins dropped. Smiling at anyone who smiled at me. The Colored Ladies would say to Betty, "L.P. is such a quiet well-behaved young man." And Betty would say, "Of course, I've raised him you know." But she wouldn't add, "He's mine."

I was hers that summer, and keeping score of days with air-conditioning and gained respect became a religion. I thought I should paint with watercolors every image: brown faces against rust-colored walls, spaceship chairs in marble plastic, mocha women bending down to bowl in toreador pants, with asses like cantaloupes in a basket, their husbands discarded for rest of these slow

Sundays, sitting in bedrooms, waiting. I realized the next time I came I would bring a book and count it all, everything that puzzled me or made me feel wanted. And I knew, temporarily, I was fine.

IT WAS THE Fourth of July, and the summer of 1968 had turned each new day potentially mean as a loose door in a high wind. Afternoon air bleached and incinerated my thoughts into a wave of my hand. Tomorrow, I would do everything I didn't do today. I was sunburned from going out in the morning. Betty wouldn't let me out in the afternoon. She was afraid I'd climb a tree, faint and fall. Or swim in a canal and be taken out into the desert, drowned.

It wasn't just me. Everyone in Phoenix knew to stay inside after one o'clock during July and August. The city became silent. Only bums and Indian women and colored people went out into the heat.

Betty was watering her garden in the middle of the day. A Kool dangled on her lip. She kept a wet handkerchief pasted on her forehead, just above her sunglasses. Her pumpkin squash were getting big and her roses were a powdery brown. When she aimed the hose at them, they shook and cracked. Leaves and shrunken buds disappeared into sand and manure.

"Goddamit," Betty mumbled. Brenda was running in a sweat, her tongue hanging, and Betty turned the hose on her. Brenda jumped in the air and shook herself. Betty spit her cigarette on the ground and turned the hose off. She looked around her garden.

"Goddamit," she mumbled again.

A broken picnic table Frank had repaired was covered with a red-and-white tablecloth made of laminated plastic and paper plates. She had placed red outdoor candles around the garden and on the table. The day before Frank had pounded four tiki torches in the yard after he mowed the razory grass. In between mowing and pounding, it was my job to pass him a big bolt of Colt 45 from the shade of the porch. He had taken his shirt off, and I wondered if his blue-black skin could be burnt, or if it just got blacker.

Frank had large nipples and a pot belly that didn't look like one, because his shoulders were so broad, when he stood up straight it disappeared. What fascinated me was the hair on his chest. It wasn't like the white hair on my grandfather's chest, which came out in long tufts, like heavy thread. Frank's was a map of tight curls that looked like spots that shouldn't be there. I wondered if Betty had to comb them out at night.

I watched his eyes redden the more he mowed, the more Colt 45 he drank. He and Betty didn't like the heat. Betty became cross with Frank over tiny things. On most hot summer night, Frank would slam the door and drive to the liquor store to buy whiskey and Colt 45, which he poured into equal amounts when he got home. When I asked to taste it, Betty shook her head "no."

"That's what grown men drink. They're fools," she added, looking at Frank, who pretended not to care, his eyes focused on the television. His favorite show, *F Troop*, was on.

"That Forrest Tucker sure is funny." He bypassed Betty's eyes and winked at me. It meant, "Sure, L.P., later you can have a sip."

But Frank always fell asleep in front of the television before I had my chance to savor whiskey and Colt 45. Betty rustled around him quietly, putting away the liquor and dinner, then touched his shoulder with the palm of her hand, and disappeared into their purple bedroom. Frank would wake up, stumble to the television, turn it off, then shuffle to Betty in the dark.

I wondered if my mother would adapt this routine with Bob, her new husband. If, as I grew, they would wear slippers and move through every night using the unspoken as a comfort. I doubted it. My mother wanted charm in her life on a constant basis. There had to be candles and high voices. Vivid sunsets.

I hadn't heard from her for a month. Betty explained this was all right, that Violet would call me soon. Sometimes I cried, but by July I began not to care. A clarity had enveloped my legs and arms. My heart followed.

I had discovered how to climb eucalyptus trees. Early

every morning, I followed Grover and Samuel to a grove
of eucalyptus bordering a deep, slow irrigation canal full
of catfish. They were better at climbing than I was.
Grover couldn't reach limbs because he was too fat, but
Samuel and I were able to climb a hundred feet or more.
From there I could see Phoenix: Camelback Mountain
and the mansions of Paradise Valley and Scottsdale, the
irrigation canals and highways and flower fields to the
south. I could even see the apartment building where I
was supposed to live.

One eucalyptus was close to the canal and we made
a practice of jumping off into the yellow-green water
when it was still, so we could scatter the catfish, their
tails and fins pulling out from under us when our feet
hit bottom. No one told us the water was filthy. For
me it was an ocean. Chinese junks were drifting by.
There were steamships in the distance. I knew somehow
that this canal led west to the ocean. That if I had to, I
could swim until I reached the Pacific.

Betty's predictions for my summer were correct. I
drifted in fiery air, discovering the tints of the new:
ebony Jesuses, Baptist temples, groves of trees and flowers, and two-lane roads with potholes and ends missing.
Phoenix didn't put as much money into the roads in
colored town because good roads were for white people.
Roads in and leading out. Roads to escape, roads to
arrive. Roads without compromise, pointing the way to
the jackpot.

When we jumped into the canal, I was a woman with
wings. I knew flight was in my life, like the whisper jets
making their descent not far from us, sleek and brightly

striped. I marveled at Grover and Samuel's skin. How clear it was, without blemishes, tightly stretched and setting sparks in the morning sun. We always wore bathing suits. The idea of jumping in naked was not allowed.

Grover told me of an older boy named Davis that played with other boys naked in the basement of his house. He said Davis was thirteen and had candy and hot dogs. Davis was already a man and things happened.

"You wanna go?" Grover looked at me and lowered his eyes.

"Davis is real important at school," Samuel added. "You being white. He'll be your friend. He doesn't know anybody white."

"I don't know," I said. The idea was frightening, but it excited me. Naked boys and games. What kind of games? If I was the center of attention and wore a sheet I might enjoy it. Like the Fall of the Roman Empire.

Summer was long. An infinity of heat and television and grape soda. We forgot about Davis for the day.

I had to leave, as Frank was setting up his tiki torches and Betty was planning the Fourth of July barbecue for us the next day. I dried myself off with a towel Betty gave me that morning. Samuel and Grover were giggling.

"You do everything like a girl, L.P.," Grover sneered.

"I think he's pretty. I want to be as pretty as L.P.," Samuel said, looking at Grover. "You're fat. You're jealous."

I had grown accustomed to Grover and Samuel. If Grover was hungry, he began calling me a girl. Samuel always came to my defense. A standoff. Then, within minutes, we would forget. I was tough. It was not the first time I'd been called names.

God allows children the gift of convenient memory. In their innocence, they do not have time to remember.

I closed my eyes, then opened them, staring into the sun, waiting for the spots.

"Don't do that," Samuel sputtered. "My mother says you'll go blind doing that!"

"So?" I retorted. My voice was full of rage. I did not understand why.

Suddenly, Samuel walked over to me and kissed me on the lips, and backed away. The three of us stood facing each other, not knowing what to say. I looked at the ground, then at the sky. It was a heave of blue, knotted and brilliant with morning. I could feel Samuel's lips on mine; they were thick, a completely different texture than my mother's, or grandmother's, and I wasn't sure I liked them. But the fact that a boy kissed me, a friend who thought I was pretty, began to excite me, and I picked up my towel, which I had dropped. Crickets were buzzing in the grove. Grover said nothing, then giggled. Samuel kicked a stone into the canal. I looked up at him.

He began to say something, then stopped, listening to the crickets. The three of us did not know if what we just did was bad, but at least we hadn't done it on Sunday. I began to laugh. Grover picked up his towel.

"I'm telling," he grumbled. Grover studied me briefly.

"You want to kiss L.P., too!" Samuel suddenly realized, laughing at him. Grover's eyes darted away from me.

"I do not!" Grover folded his towel.

Fields of weeds and eucalyptus groves are full of mercy in the wrong part of town, and suddenly we forgot about Samuel's kiss. A desert jackrabbit hopped in front of us from some still green tumbleweeds. Samuel screamed. Grover tried to jump it and fell down. When he got up, I looked at him.

"Frank's bought fireworks for the Fourth of July." I chewed a butterscotch and offered him one. He took it. With this gesture I knew we still had secrets. Grover and I began to walk along the canal, through pockets of flies and river reeds, and Samuel followed.

"You want to fish for catfish on Saturday?" Grover asked in a hoarse whisper. That was two days away.

"Sure," I said.

"You can eat them. They're very sweet. My mother loves them." Grover sounded earnest, thrilled at the idea. He could have fun and please Marcelline.

"Catfish eat fish poop," Samuel said. "My mother says only lower-class Negroes eat catfish."

"Do catfish look like cats?" I asked. I knew Grover would hit Samuel in a second.

"They have whiskers," Grover offered, looking past Samuel. He kept his eyes on the two-lane vacant highway three hundred yards ahead of us. From there we would walk along the highway back to South Phoenix and its square, tiny yards fronting cement bungalows with air coolers humming on roofs. They shimmered a mile away, creating their own liquid in the air above them. The highway would be hot, surrounded by desert, saguaros and the occasional manzanita tree. We would keep our faces to the ground, walk deliberately at a pace so we wouldn't tire or faint. This was the part of going back to Betty that I liked. I thought of Peter O'Toole and *Lawrence of Arabia*. I arranged my white towel on my shoulders and head to look just like him. I prayed for a desert wind and dust. I would lead us home from the Sahara into Cairo and everyone would applaud. But I thought more of what a black boy's kiss tasted like, and the satisfied shock of its intent.

The three of us walked with towels over our heads, three minutes from noon, fifteen minutes from home, and it was my home this summer; like a tent in the desert, Betty turning her chicken over in a pail of barbecue sauce and lemons, mountains full of copper and resin shifting behind her, in a place where there are no roads.

We were beginning to sweat under our towels. Grover panted.

"We're almost there," he repeated every six, seven steps. Samuel tried to hold my hand, but I brushed it away, then smiled at him from under my towel.

I saw only a road in. Without redemption or cars moving out, this road measured itself in my sunburnt steps, my dark companions with white eyes and yellow rims, who thought I was pretty, worth fighting over perhaps, and suddenly, in the onion-colored stream, it seemed to me this was the road I was meant to walk.

At dusk the doorbell rang. Betty was wearing red, white, and blue slacks and a white shirt rolled up to the elbows. She had made sure every shade was down, the air cooler and fans blowing; the house was cool and lavender, beckoning with a bar with an ice bucket and barbecue smoke drifting from the backyard. I felt very American.

Frank was wearing a checked red, white, and blue short-sleeved shirt and a bow tie. His arms were too muscular for his shirt and the sleeves rolled up to his shoulders every time he moved his arms. My job was to hold a tray of different drinks, already poured and full of ice. Betty had poured a fifth of vodka into some Hi-C punch and mixed that with lemonade. My tray had five cups of this punch, three root beers, and two short tub glasses with bourbon on crushed ice. I could smell the bourbon and I liked it. It reminded me of my grand-father's friends.

Betty waved me over to stand next to her as she opened the door.

"Stand still and smile, and don't giggle or spill the drinks," she cautioned. I did as I was told.

Betty opened the door and heat blew through my shirt. Marcelline and Grover stepped in, Marcelline ooh-ing over Betty's outfit. Marcelline then walked over to me.

"You look adorable, honey." She peered at the tray and sniffed at the liquors, then hesitated, like she was selecting a chocolate. She picked the punch, then handed Grover a root beer. I remembered someone else who sniffed and picked like this. It was Jean Harlow in *Dinner at Eight*, only she was in a white satin bed and she took the chocolate she didn't like out of her mouth and put it back in the box. I wondered if Marcelline would put her drink back on my tray after she tasted it.

"Where's William?" I whispered to Grover.

"Mother and William broke up. She's got a new boy-friend now." He cocked his head and I saw a fat, light-skinned colored man in a golf outfit come in. He had very white teeth and a white fedora hat. There were gold rings with diamond chips on half his available fin-gers. He laughed before he spoke. This worried me. People who laugh before they speak are not to be trusted, because everything coming out of their mouths is the end of a joke, or leading up to one. I knew people who slapped each other on the back and spoke in jokes, also spoke in riddles, and were willing to deceive.

Everyone arrived at once. They knew Betty well enough to assess her dislike of the inappropriate. One of these dislikes was being late. Betty never wore a watch, but went through life placing wall clocks and asking sympathetic people the time; it was a fetish that became easy with practice, and she was always on time. My grandmother used to infuriate Betty.

Georgia never gave a damn about the time. She got up when she wanted to, went to lunch at odd hours, often forgot to come home by five on Betty's payday. I would hear Betty muttering in that pale blue apartment, wiping down the kitchen counter for the twentieth time, then Georgia would sweep in with cash for Betty and a silver or turquoise caftan just for her. Betty would never know what to say after receiving such a lovely gift, and I knew my grandmother always understood exactly what she was doing.

In the bright haze of the doorway, Samuel was a silhouette who assumed form inside, then his mother with her rhinestone glasses.

"Lucille, you look wonderful. Why I would never have known you'd been unwell." Betty hugged Lucille and turned to another fat colored man who came in behind her.

"Armando." This was all Betty said, as though speaking his name in a slightly pious voice was enough. I realized I had heard her speak about Lucille's various and continuing illnesses before, and that Lucille would probably stay sick her entire life, as a point of safe conversation with her friends, which were few, and that Armando was spoken of as a saint. He didn't look like a saint. He looked like one of the bears from a Walt Disney nature film.

I realized, holding that tray as people grabbed for glasses in the purple shadows, that I was beginning to grow up. I was able to discern histories from a simple inflection in the voice, and also know that certain people were not to be trusted, just from a laugh. I had already learned not to trust my mother or grandmother. But I had assumed the outside world, away from school and apartments with bitter air, must have had something in which to place faith. I was wrong.

Lucille and Armando were standing in front of someone who I couldn't make out. The silhouette looked like a girl, but I only saw the fuzz of a long, pale summer around her.

As Lucille whisked up a punch and peered at me through pinched, lurid little eyes, I backed a step. She looked like she was always ready to hit something, that

a nerve was cut and made her mean. She sat down,
crossed her legs, stood up, sat down again. She slapped
her husband on the shoulder and gestured curtly for a
cigarette, which he lit then passed over to her. She took
two puffs, then stubbed it out in the ashtray, and drank
all her punch. She kept her eyes on Samuel, nodded to
me for another drink, then spoke in a high, thin chirp.

"Where's Aisha?"

"I'm right here, Mama." The figure outside had become a fifteen-year-old girl with bad skin and brilliant
yellow eyes. She already had very large breasts, and in
her blue cotton dress, she looked like she, too, didn't
belong here.

I thought Aisha very exotic and beautiful. Her name
was for a princess. She looked at me and smiled.

"Do I get my choice?" I saw silver rings and bracelets
on her fingers as she went over the drinks on my tray.

"Root beer," I murmured, keeping my eyes on the
floor.

"Uh-uh." When I lifted my eyes, she had already
downed a glass of Betty's punch and then politely took
a root beer.

"What's your name?" she asked me in a conspirato-
rial tone.

"L.P.," I murmured, wanting to smile and not sure
if I should.

"Your real name?" She lifted my chin.

"Lindsay Paul. No one calls me that, though." I had
never seen eyes so completely yellow. If the Indian
women had seen her they would have whispered, "Cat,
cat," and signaled each other with their hands.

"You're cute, L.P." She winked at me and walked on.
Then a man hovered over me. He was towering and
gaunt. He wore a beret and carried a musician's black
case. He didn't even smile at me as he walked in, but
he took a drink.

"Hey baby, what's news?" It was Betty's voice coming at him. She walked differently, very sexy, and held
out her hand for this specter to kiss. It was very dramatic,
and I knew by the tone in her voice this was from the
past, her very own past, that no one could walk into. It
must be show business, I thought, and I was right.

On the musician's black case was the word SKELETON,
written in fancy red and pink letters, with a skull and
crossbones above them. His hands were terribly dry, and
they shook.

"Look, everyone, it's my old baby, Herbie Skeleton
Powell, and the most beautiful trumpet this side of
heaven." Betty made a broad gesture with her hands.
Everyone stood up and came over to shake this half-
dead man's hands. Obviously this man was famous.

"I saw you play with Tex Beneke, the Count Basie!"
Larry, the joke man, was laughing, shaking Skeleton's
hand.

"Long time ago, man. Now Miles Davis on the West
Coast," Skeleton whispered. He drank quickly, but his
voice was like the desert. A wind that came from nowhere, then died.

"Trying to get Betty to come back, do a couple of
tunes. Vinyl."

He turned and looked at Betty. The room went silent.

Frank scowled. I realized my drink tray was empty and I put it on the floor.

In that moment, I saw everyone in cool mauve shadows, rattling the ice in their drinks, listening, waiting, like darts. My eyes turned blank, like the moment before I closed them, after staring into intense light, and Betty's small frame began to sway slightly. I imagined her in hotels with the drapes drawn, in Hollywood and New York and Chicago, with flowers and music and makeup. And I wondered what it must be like to live at night, in clubs and recording studios and hotel rooms with shades.

This bungalow was kept dark, not to keep the heat and sunlight out, but to keep the shadows in. Betty seemed to understand how to move in shade, make decisions, keep her life ordered. Shadows must be memory, I thought, and Betty looked into them, just like I did light, to create her language. Her own colors and indistinct words, foreign to the present, dated but not unkind. Shadows only frightened me. I believe they were fine to hide in, but not friendly. That if I stood too long in them, or tried to understand why they were there, claws would pull me in, like I had seen on *The Twilight Zone*. That is why the Indian women never sat too long in the shade. They used shadows to cool themselves, cook, rest, but then they walked back into the sun, never hiding their faces.

The air in Betty's living room was lightly scented with charcoal smoke coming from the backyard, Marcelline's Tigress perfume, and Larry's hair pomade, a coconut oil that stained the collar of his shirt. And cigars. Frank smoked cigars on special days like the Fourth of July.

Aisha slumped onto the plastic-covered sofa and watched me, then turned her gaze to her mother's back and frowned. Lucille was standing still, but I noticed her hands digging into Samuel's shoulder. Samuel stared at the floor. Grover stood next to him and put his foot on Samuel's and pressed down, knowing this was an adult silence, and if Samuel yelled, Lucille would slap him.

I realized Betty was listening to a music I couldn't see or explain, that her eyes never left Skeleton. She smiled weakly, then looked at Frank and began to sigh, breaking the silence.

"God, I'm hungry. Frank, you start up the chicken and I'll fix some more punch. It's good to see you, Skeleton."

I suddenly knew she wouldn't go back to Hollywood. That if she did, Frank would leave her. I didn't understand why anyone would leave Betty. If the leaving had to be done, I imagined she would be the one to do it.

There was laughter. Our relieved guests circled Skeleton and chatted. Skeleton nodded his head and spoke in monosyllables. He never put down his case.

In the kitchen, I saw Betty staring at Frank. He started to walk toward her. She put her hand up in a violent, noiseless gesture, and he stopped. Frank quietly opened the screen door and walked out to the barbecue. Grover and Samuel ignored me, and raced through the kitchen to the back. I could see them jumping up and down through the smoke, then coughing.

Betty wasn't laughing with everyone in the living room. She stood at the kitchen window, but she wasn't looking out at anything. Her face was smooth and reckless. I knew she wanted to go, but I was keeping her here. And I was furious with my mother for making me a burden to someone else. Betty touched the window-pane. She was talking to God. Asking what was appropriate, if there were still prophecies left, if she was too old. She was waiting on the Fourth of July for a sign and there weren't any, and she knew it. She opened a bottle of vodka and poured it in the punch bowl. There weren't any shadows in the kitchen.

The sun whispered summer and died. Night was going to be dry indigo, windless, and we were going to sweat. Frank lit the tiki torches and Lucille applauded.

The adults were quite drunk. They steadily drank until the vodka and punch ran out, then Betty decided to make Manhattans. There was a bluejay who kept flying down, trying to get bits of food off the table. Betty swatted at him, but he kept coming until darkness seeped into the sky. I had eaten a lot and I felt tired. I tried barbecue chicken and ham hocks with collard greens, homemade potato chips, potato salad, Shrimp Louie, hot dogs, and two slices of Key Lime pie.

Samuel watched me, and the flicker of the tiki torches made him look mean, so I ignored him. Grover was asleep on Betty's aluminum chaise lounge, which broke under him and he still stayed asleep. I heard Betty and Frank laughing.

Something had broken in the summer night sky. As if air had turned into another element, a gas or a precious metal, and we were not responsible. I listened to the adults laughing, and tried to break the codes. I tried to laugh like an adult. I began to see that when children laugh, it's because something is violent or funny or new. But when an adult laughs, it's from relief.

I tried to mimic Betty and Marcelline's melodic chirps, their giggles smoothing out their night into something fragrant and safe. They sounded like night birds. I surmised I'd never seen a night bird. And that Betty and Marcelline's dark hands could flutter through the night, perfect, invisible, weightless. They would be able to fly, build nests, sing at midnight, and no one would know.

I wondered where Aisha was. Then I saw her. She was near the chain-link fence in the back, which was covered with passion flower vine and weeds. I could see her eyes in the dark. She was rummaging in her bag, then playing with her silver rings. I sat down next to her.

Her back stiffened. I noticed her ears had five tiny pierced earrings running up each lobe. She turned and smiled at me, then cracked her knuckles, rearranging all her silver rings so they were face-up on her fingers. Some were too big and dropped around sideways.

"You should be a girl, L.P. You're so delicate." I was going to get up and go. I got tired of these analogies. Aisha grabbed my elbow and motioned for me to stay.

"Don't get upset. See, I know these things. I'm a witch." She nodded her head, satisfied.

"Next year, when I'm sixteen, I'm going to split Phoenix." Aisha watched for my reaction. Her face didn't seem so acned or female in the glow of the fire.

"To New Orleans. That's where the men are. And

us witches. See, I said this about you 'cause somewhere in your past you was a beautiful woman."

I gave this some thought, then looked into the amber of her eyes.

"Like Sophia Loren?" I asked. This made sense.

"Could be," she sniffed, "but I'm not sure. I'll know in a minute."

"What do you mean?" I noticed the smile on her face was coming out of her like oil from the ground.

"Yeh, there we *go*." Aisha turned to me and I could see her pupils had dilated. There was no yellow.

"Now we's tripping."

"What?" I wondered if she was a hippie witch.

Aisha looked in her bag and pulled out a tiny square piece of paper with a stain on it.

"See this? It's blotter acid. This is how you become a witch. I'm going to marry Jimi Hendrix. Cast a spell on *him,* babay."

Aisha lay down on the ground and looked up at the sky.

"Bitchin'." She put her arms behind her head.

I lay down with her.

"What about a past life? How do we do that?" I asked. For me, the idea of more than one life was completely new territory. I had to understand it immediately or I would die.

"Look, L.P. Big Dipper. Little Dipper. Bitchin'." Her hand waved through the smoke of the barbecue's last embers. We could hear the adults laughing hysterically.

"You go through lots a lives till the spirits say you

ready to be one of them. Then that's it." Aisha turned and stared at me like I was a dream.

"Light me a cigarette, L.P. They's in my bag." I had never smoked a cigarette, and I knew now, in the darkness, I could if I wanted to. I looked in Aisha's bag, expecting to find witch things, like small animals and eyes, but it was just a teenage girl's bag, filled with Woolworth's cosmetics and pink gym socks and a pack of Marlboros.

I took one out, struck a match and lit it. I didn't cough. It tasted good, like happy rooms and places where adults laughed. I handed it to Aisha, relieved she had not asked me to try blotter acid. At the gas station the attendants had to use gloves when they tested the battery on Georgia's Cadillac, and anything that required gloves I didn't want in my stomach.

"You and me, we knew each other in Egypt." Aisha rolled her head around on the grass and smoked. "We switched places now, see. I was a king, you was a slave girl." I blinked.

"Or something like that." Aisha frowned, then concentrated on the sky.

Lying next to the witch, I considered I had never noticed how much larger the sky becomes at night. That I could see all of it from horizon to horizon, its blue varnish shiny and hard.

The adults had stopped laughing and I listened to the crack and whir of the tiki torches. It was too quiet. Something was going to happen. I wondered if Betty and Frank were fighting.

Then the sound of a trumpet, very high, like a siren. And the slow beat of a jazz song. Skeleton was playing.

Aisha pointed to the sky. There, in its pit, began a series of fireworks, in yellow and purple and white, bursting in mushroom clouds, like my blind spots, burning into the night.

Aisha hummed, and suddenly I realized she had fallen asleep. Betty wouldn't sing tonight, though she had sung at church, and I listened for a thought of a song to come to her. Maybe she would rustle uncomfortably on the picnic bench, or stand on the porch, behind mended screens, deliberately away from the others, fireworks illuminating her face. And she would sing like in the movies.

But Betty sat quietly, watching with her guests a sky momentarily littered with electric blooms and occasional thunder from cherry bombs. Skeleton's sweet horn played no particular song at all, as natural as visits from the past that become occasional magic. Lying on the scratchy lawn with Aisha, a grasshopper on my chest and a cigarette in my shirt pocket, I felt dizzy, completely and utterly alone. And this felt like the world was in balance, that being alone was not being lonely.

My mother was traveling and I didn't know where. My grandmother was in Europe and I didn't know where. I was with a witch who would move to New Orleans and remember me years later in her cards and incantations. I knew Betty wasn't going anywhere, and that made me happy. I knew Grover and Samuel wouldn't tell about a wet morning kiss, that the eucalyptus groves were our desert. Not tomorrow, but the day after, and the day after that, and tonight was an acid dream, asleep in its comfort and display. I counted fireworks. I counted them until someone could remember where I was.

eleven

PRAYERS ARE SPOKEN on knees next to a bed, in the anonymity of church pews, quiet rooms. Prayers are sometimes selfish, asking, demanding assurances. I was taught never to ask for anything, because God wouldn't grant personal wishes, but to ask for strength, kindness, and love.

Wishes were only good at wishing ponds, birthday cakes with lit candles, four-leaf clovers, and Buddhas. There I could ask for the world if I wanted it. I always asked for the same thing. To be real, like everyone else, but I knew that was an impossibility. I was not a real boy, but a creature in between, which precluded contact with other boys until I had figured them out.

I was taught to pray each night before bed, then once in the morning as a clear start, like cleaning my teeth before breakfast. Prayers in the morning were hurried, and repetitive, and meant nothing to me.

Today, a week after the Fourth of July, in a hundred degree heat, at 9:00 A.M., I prayed that Violet would be home soon, or at least call. I still hadn't heard from her, and Betty refused to discuss the subject. I made my prayer more important to God so He would get my message, and I even got down on my knees.

I knew Betty was taking me to the apartments to do some cleaning. She asked me if I needed anything from my room on the third floor, and I said I wasn't sure. But I wanted to go.

It took us a long time to get started. Betty had to put on her uniform, because colored ladies were not allowed in my apartment building without their uniforms on. The rich white women would throw fits if they saw a Negro in their building with regular clothes on. Entree to this private realm meant uniforms, special cards stating who they worked for, names, social security numbers, addresses. Even for the maids who had worked there for years.

I was wearing shorts, thongs, and a Hawaiian shirt with surfers on it when we rang the back door of the apartment building.

"Don't you have a key?" I asked Betty.

"No, honey. Your grandmother forgot to leave me one." Betty kept her hand over her forehead. She said when the heat hit her forehead she got headaches.

"I've got one," I offered, searching in my shorts pockets. I knew my grandmother would never give Betty a key, that she was covering it for me.

When I pulled it out, she stared at me in surprise.

"You didn't tell me."

"I forgot." I really did. I spent most of my time in the eucalyptus groves. Grover and Samuel and I had built a house of particle board we found in a garbage dump. We played *Gilligan's Island*. Samuel was the professor. Grover was the Skipper. I was Ginger. The key stayed in a box under my bed on the porch. Along with money and white people's things.

I shrugged and reached up to put the key in the back door. A doorman that I didn't recognize came up from behind the door. He looked at Betty, then looked from behind the glass down at me. As I began to twist the knob, I could feel him keep it locked on the other side. It was boiling, and I wanted to get in the air-conditioning. I was furious.

The doorman tapped his hand on the glass, gesturing for Betty to show her card, which she did, sullen and squinting, one leg jutted out. This doorman, about thirty, with moles on his cheek and a toothpick in his mouth, let us in.

"Got to show your card." He stared down at me. I was getting madder. This was my home. How dare he?

"Who's the kid? This building doesn't allow kids."

"I live here!" I screamed.

Betty stepped in front of me, and her voice became very sweet, a new voice that sounded stupid, but practiced, and I realized she used this voice before, to get things accomplished with white men. She used this voice just to be allowed. And it was an entirely separate language.

"Yes, they do." She read his name tag. "Jim. You must be the summer replacement for Harley. This is L.P." Gracefully, Betty brought me around by my shoulders, facing him.

"So? I don't know this." He didn't like us.

"Then you call Mr. Powell, the manager. He'll explain." Her voice was still very sweet, but I could tell she was annoyed. "Just tell him L.P. Fowler's here with Betty. He's the grandson of the Fowlers. He lives on the third floor. They own three apartments in this building, Jim." Her voice had dropped to a reverential whisper.

Jim scratched his cheek. I hated him.

"Okay. You both stay here while I make the call." I realized he was stupid. He didn't know this building was mine. That I played by myself on the roof garden on the top, dangling my legs over the edge with no railing and I wasn't frightened at all. Betty and I stood for a long time by the elevator, waiting. I saw she wasn't half as embarrassed as I, and realized that she must spend half her life waiting to be let in by white people.

Jim came back and smiled, shaking my hand.

"Boy, was I wrong! Well, L.P. I hope you aren't too mad at me?" He bent down and looked into my eyes. I could smell bologna sandwich on him. I deliberately ignored him and turned to Betty.

"Betty, I'm thirsty. Can we go upstairs now and get a drink?" I punched the elevator button and the doors opened. We got inside. Jim made a half-hearted wave. The doors closed.

Betty began to laugh so hard she shook.

"Baby doll, you are your grandmother's grandson, that is for sure!" There was a front elevator, but children and help weren't allowed on that. Unless they were with the owners. And then I would have to wear a coat and tie. I hated the front elevator with its flat little chandelier and crisscrossed carpeting.

On the ninth floor we let ourselves into Georgia's pink kitchen. Shades were down, and the apartment was freezing. Betty sat down at the kitchen table, something I'd never seen her do, and brought out a list of things she had to finish. She lit a Kool.

I walked through the blue rooms and touched the heavy French furniture as I had, it seemed, thousands of times. Suddenly I felt that it wasn't mine; I was a stranger looking in, like a thief, at someone else's life. I became very cold. When I turned around, Betty stood watching me, her arms crossed.

"Funny, isn't it, L.P.? When no one's around. Makes you wonder if you lived here at all. Empty rooms. They show what we don't know."

"Are they ever coming back?" The idea that they might not terrified me. Betty uncrossed her arms and picked up a bottle of apple juice.

"This should have been put back in the icebox. It's gone bad." Betty made a pinched face when she opened the cap, then poured the apple juice down the sink. She had to give me answers. I asked her again.

"Are they ever coming back?"

Betty looked at me with an impatient twitch.

"L.P., that is really a stupid question. Of course they're coming back. What's the matter? Aren't you happy staying with Frank and me?" she asked, with smooth annoyance.

"Sure," I answered. The idea of whether or not I was happy never seemed important. Everyone else's happiness always seemed the big priority. I looked around. Georgia's apartment was much smaller than I thought. My grandmother made the apartment big.

"It's you and me this summer." Betty left this remark on a short breath, as if she meant to say more, but decided against it, and she walked over to my grandmother's baby grand and sat down. She touched a high key, looking out at the view. It sounded like night birds that always woke up two hours before dawn, and cried in short, unconnected songs.

"I wish it could be this way all the time, L.P. I really do." Betty touched her hair. I didn't understand her reasoning, and I was scared. She didn't look at me anymore, but stared out through the picture window, too large for a shade. Had Betty said this to me in her house, I would have half listened, but here it was eerie. Maybe I was destined to live with Betty from now on. Maybe no one had bothered to tell me.

The thought of living with Betty punched me for a moment. I could be poor, like her. I knew it was only a matter of thinking about different things, instead of money and how to spend it. I could navigate the loss, bend, and grow with darkened skin into someone tall and grave and masculine.

Maybe I had black blood in me. Maybe my mother didn't tell me, but now that it was noticeable, she and Georgia were getting rid of me. Maybe I was Betty's son by a white man and that visit from my father, when I was five, was theater. Such intrigue appealed to me, but I knew I was wrong.

"God, I hate this place." Betty touched another chord of the piano as she said this.

"Hate what? Phoenix or here?" I pointed to the living room.

"Both," Betty said quietly. She began to play the piano. It was classical music. I was shocked. I knew Betty liked jazz, boogie woogie, country and western music. But classical music. It certainly fit the dark apartment.

"I went to the finest conservatory in Baltimore, when I was not much older than you, L.P. Look where it got me." She began to play an intricate piece with a delicate, calculating hand.

What I saw was a hump-backed, green-eyed black women in a starched white uniform, sitting at a baby grand piano. She was playing Chopin in her employer's apartment, vacant enough for an echo.

The sun had tanned me darker than Betty. I stepped forward, to the same spot where Georgia normally put her hand on her hip, in that desperate part of her day when she thought no one was looking, when she stared out her picture window. Above this hot city she despised, Georgia plotted, manufacturing her cruelties for the week ahead. She would touch the back of her pulled-up hair to make sure it was in place, and promised herself she would survive.

I put my hand on my hip, like Georgia, touched the back of my head and stared out the picture window, trying to think and feel what she did. Perhaps, if I moved the right way, thought the right things, I would see the world as she saw it.

The city below was silent as we were. Betty quickly played her classical music, letting each key slowly resonate. Phoenix was waiting, as we were, for something foreign to pass over it. There were no clouds in the sky. Only a tambourine wind and the stench of the sun.

I turned to Betty and dropped my hand from my hip.

"I got the keys to 3-B, Betty. I'll go down and check on stuff."

Betty focused on me and stopped playing.

"Now that's being a real gentleman, L.P. Half an hour, no more."

The air-conditioning turned itself off. I saw familiar patterns of dust in the barricaded air, not falling down to cover tables and velvet pillows, but suspended in a half light, waiting for Violet and Georgia to stir it up, wave it around with anger. Betty seemed to know this half light. This wasn't her first piano in a closed room.

I got out my keys.

"You should sing again, Betty."

"What?" This caught her. Her voice was a yelp.

I shuffled my thongs in the rug till they bent.

"Well. You like singing. And you play the piano." I heard my voice. I sounded stupid and condescending. I felt very short and foolish.

"Oh, L.P. Go on down to 3-B." She smiled, then shooed me, turning her attention to her list.

I opened the door to 3-B. I turned on a light. I felt that I should be walking through a cavern full of stalactites and stalagmites, a sound of water dripping, bats ready to swoop.

Then I pretended I was a ghost coming back to spy on the living. Nothing was alive here. I began to cry. My glass horses and photographs of Marilyn Monroe and Sophia Loren didn't seem like much at all.

I was not there. I looked for a trace of my own smell. Or Violet's perfume. Nothing. There was cheap tainted odor of air mist deodorizer, mothballs, and sachets. The same scent as my grandmother's closets. Georgia had taken over my room when I wasn't there, and it was unfair.

I walked into my dark room and turned on a light, not opening the shades. I put my hands in the pockets of my shorts. I counted to ten, thinking what I might need for the rest of my summer, what was in this room. I ran my hands over the glass on top of my small black desk. Nothing here was important. I turned off the light.

In my mother's bedroom I became my own ghost. I turned the lights on. She had put new drapes up, aqua silk, and an aqua silk bedspread fluffed with aqua silk pillows. There were jade roses and photographs of my mother with Bob in silver-and-wood frames. Her photos of me had been taken down and stacked on a shelf. I turned the light off.

I was dead now. Someone else came and took my place. She must have waited and planned for me to be gone, to create this new decor. Planning behind my back so she could get it done in a day, before she left on her honeymoon. It only took a day. And it must have taken only minutes to put my photographs in a stack on a lower shelf.

I stood paralyzed in the pulsing afternoon dark, and thought about what the dead must feel. They don't feel things the way the living do, but they connect, touching the living for electricity. I imagined the dead move with barren arms, flames on their palms, waiting for the right womb. And God says, there are no guarantees, it's a matter of black and red and roulette but all of you are so hungry. So be it. You fly, you see the answers and your intentions are eternal. You want to live over again. I'll make some of you trees. I'll make some of you dogs and fish. Some of you will die young, some of you will die old and mean. And you will be right back with me, rubbing your palms together so you get the fire and can see.

The dead watch children closely, hover and feed. And when a child cries, they do nothing. They know they soon will be born and come out wailing, a crucified red, soft as the heart meat of a fig. And the genius is they remember nothing.

On that day in July I began to forget. I learned in the dark hall of my own apartment how the living and dead occupy rooms together, that objects and furniture and colors are meaningless without the soul that assigns them their use. At the front door I took a candy, like guests do, a peppermint, murmured a prayer that was too confused, too fast, too demanding, and walked back into my summer.

twelve

ON AUGUST 5 I developed a high fever that lasted one night. This was not uncommon, but Betty was terrified. She wouldn't let Frank on the back porch. She fed me aspirin and vitamin C every hour, covered my head with wet eucalyptus leaves and handkerchiefs full of ice.

I dreamed, remembering everything. These were not fever dreams, which hold insanity and visions in their mouths, like a goldfish, popping out nightmares underwater. These dreams were exact and calculated.

My fever had reached one hundred and four and my teeth were chattering when I began to close my eyes. I could hear Betty's voice on the telephone, talking to a doctor. I could smell the aroma of her Kools. It was a hundred and four outside, and I was the same temperature as the city. Then a rosy black. Betty later told me I fell asleep with my arms outstretched in the air.

It began with fire. There was a fire in the post office and gifts and letters my family had sent to me were lost. The postal ladies were on roller skates, trying to skate their way out of the burning post office, but they were trapped. They began to scream, turning their faces to look at me, saying, "L.P., we couldn't help it, your parcels, the fire, we can't get out!"

I was in a white Cadillac with wings. Marcelline and Grover and I were flying above a cow field and Marcelline was laughing. "Don't tell Betty," she whispered. Grover dropped bombs on the cow field, a mile below us, and he had an aviator's hat on. He told me he was the king of England. I asked if I could be queen.

I leaned over to watch the cattle scatter in fiery fields, some running in circles, others knocking down fences, braying. Marcelline circled the Cadillac and began to dive down. I fell out, and as I fell, I thought to myself, "No, no, my mama told me if I hit the ground I wouldn't ever wake up."

I closed my eyes and pushed through my neck, and I felt wings growing through my back, covered with a slime that flew off in bits through smokey wind. Suddenly the feeling of being suspended, hung on a string, and I looked behind me and saw dragonfly wings smacking together in a wet buzz, faster than a hummingbird's, and I began to laugh.

It was the laughter of delight. I saw lights in this dreamed sky, momentarily blurred in the smoke of Grover's bombs and screams of cattle below. I could smell burning meat, and it smelled like Betty's Fourth of July barbecue, only sweeter, because the meat burning below me was alive.

I looked at the lights and I saw hands motioning to me to follow. They were other flying things; children with butterfly wings and parrots and eagles. I pushed again through my neck, and I flew up.

I became surrounded in a blue as bright and polished as a new car.

I opened my eyes and saw Betty's face over me. She was changing the ice in my handkerchief. I had burned it into a puddle on my pillow. Betty's eyes were grim. I fell back into the hard, cannibal blue.

The scene shifted. My grandmother was on her cruise ship with Henry Adams and they skirted icebergs in the North Atlantic. The wind felt cold and they weren't even walking on the deck because it was too slick. I flew through a round window into the dining room and I saw them.

Georgia made sure they ate at the captain's table. She dressed three times a day for the promenade, for shopping in the gift boutiques, for other women to see just how rich she was.

She had taken fourteen furs; I remembered, buzzing quietly above and around her, that I counted her furs the day she packed them, weeks before she was ready for the trip. Like Betty, she explained to me a woman of quality must be prepared in advance. They had been all over bedspreads and hanging on satin hangers on doorways, moving lightly in the air conditioning. Hovering over her, I desperately wanted that air-conditioning. Everything seemed so hot, even in the North Atlantic.

Georgia deliberately chose a cold place, Scandinavia, so she could dress up in furs and her best Washington clothes. She repeated to me that Phoenix was dull and hot and common. She had sable swing coats and white fox stoles. There were beige mink stoles with pockets, and gloves with baby seal, knee length stone martens with huge rhinestone buttons and matching hats. There was a full-length chinchilla for the evening with its own oversized muff. Each in their own cloth sack, like occupants in a morgue.

Her white fox stole was enormous and hung back on her chair. The fox heads were alive, snapping at flies as my grandmother chattered and ate with her mouth open. I bent down to touch one of the foxes and it tried to bite me. Then she swatted at me like I was a fly.

"Not now, L.P. I'm trying to eat."

In this dream she was taking a ship that I thought was the *Queen Mary* or the *Queen Elizabeth,* but I read on the life-rings the words "Queen of Hearts." Her dinner table was full of cigar smoke and champagne. Georgia stopped eating and only smiled, feeling like that queen, as my grandfather, his eyesight failing, poked tentatively at his lobster Newburg, pushing some of the sauce over the side of its porcelain baking dish. My grandmother let him make a mess of himself, spilling the contents of the plate on his lap, missing his mouth with his shaking champagne glass. Her face was flat. She held a heart with focused eyes, looking at me, but they were made of card. She couldn't smile because she was painted on.

But she could speak.

"I don't love you, L.P. And I'm never coming back. We are sailing around the world, and when we tire of that, we are sailing to the moon. I will be the richest woman on the moon, and I don't love you. I only say I do because of your retarded mother, and I don't even love her. I think you are both the same. Evil, cruel, stupid children. Remember, I said all this will be yours someday? It was a lie, L.P. You aren't worthy. You are a mistake of God. You are a freak of nature and you will go to hell for your sins. You will never have children and I don't love you. Do you hear me? Get off my ship. Quit flying around me. Go back to the desert. Go!"

The ship rocks and I try to find an open window, but they have slammed shut. My wings beat faster and I realize the wallpaper is Chinese, painted with dragonflies and goldfish, and I fly against it, trying to disappear. The boat rocks again. I see my grandmother's chair has straps on it, and she is bound. As the boat tilts, her chair slides into a shadow with claws. She screams out at me.

"Your mother wishes you were never born! She despises you. You are a stone around her neck. You are a waste. You are never to be called ours."

Before Georgia disappears into the far end of the room, where the shadows are, she screams out, "Henry Adams!" and I see the white fox blow around her neck, heads wiggling, mouths open.

I turn and watch my grandfather, and come away from the wall. His eyesight has improved. There is a new plate of lobster in front of him, and he is eating with an appetite. He doesn't hear or see Georgia slip and roll into the night. He can't see me, but I know he senses that I am there.

He laughs like a young man, notices the dragonfly wallpaper in the dining room, and comments to an attractive young woman across the table how beautiful dragonflies can be when you're fishing, early in the morning, on a quiet lake. They land on still water and the fish come up to bite.

I fly in circles above him, humming. Henry Adams Fowler speaks again.

"I used to catch fish with a blind man," he confides, "and he said when a lake was still, just before dawn, he could hear the fish swim up to catch the dragonflies. He said he could hear the rustle of fins, and dragonfly wings, a mile away. We caught a lot of fish together."

He is grinning at his charmed companion, a woman whose face changes from Sophia Loren to Elizabeth Taylor to my mother's face as a child.

As he laughs and drinks his champagne, his hair grows back and it is black as ground fresh pepper. The ship lurches and heels itself like a dog. The window I came in flies open. My grandmother's chair rolls back from the shadows, into place at the table. I find my way out, my translucent wings changing to purple and gold. I see other children with my same wings bursting out of the ship, into the seamless ocean light, like Fourth of July fireworks. I realize they are also checking on families who have forgotten them, navigating what was once tainted and crucified, suddenly free, suddenly transformed.

I turn to see my grandparents a last time, because I know in this dream they will never come back. My grandfather is old and half blind once more. My grandmother is rattling her diamond-and-sapphire bracelets as she makes a point to the captain. My grandfather's beautiful companion has vanished.

Perhaps this companion, this pretty woman, is my mother. She is still not grown up. She still hasn't met Leo, left my grandmother, had me, met Bob. Perhaps she hasn't been born. That is why her face continually changes, as though seen through thick bottle glass, and her silence is because she can't speak. She can laugh, pay attention to everything she adores, but she is not allowed to speak. Where I have dragonfly wings, she is merely air and image molded with unsteady hands.

"Stupid girl. You aren't alive yet!"

My grandmother slams her menu on the table and a mirror cracks from its reverberation.

Sea air is tussling my hair, the powder on my wings, which smells like celery and Coca-Cola. I push again, through my head, my neck turning red. My wings flap. I ascend.

Now I am in a night sky washed by flame and I am flying. I want to find my mother, but the school I fly in will not allow it. My wings are getting heavy, and I ask if we are in Phoenix yet. When do we get to Phoenix? I hear only a buzz of wings and their powder becomes clouds. They say, "Keep flying and never worry about touching the earth. When you touch the earth is where your problems begin."

★　　★　　★

Betty was standing over me with a branch of eucalyptus and a bottle of aspirin when I opened my eyes. I weakly laughed.

"Your fever is broken." She said this quietly. She looked exhausted, and lit a Kool, sitting down in the chair next to my red sheets.

"L.P., we thought you'd have to go to the hospital. I thought I'd have to call your Mama and make her come back from her honeymoon. But you pulled through."

It was morning. Heat came through the broken screens of the back porch in an orange grid, like soft, tiny prison bars. I looked up at Betty; I hadn't realized she'd had my mother's telephone number all along, and I wondered whose side she was on. Betty lifted me up and changed my pillowcases.

I saw Brenda outside, sniffing in circles. She squatted and peed on Betty's best flower bed. Betty saw it, too. She bolted from me, slammed the screen door, and chased Brenda away.

{ *thirteen* }

A WEEK HAD passed since I'd had wings. I was allowed to play in the eucalyptus trees but not swim in the canal, as Betty discerned its dirty water gave me fever. I had tried to explain it wasn't the canal water, that I had unexplained fevers, but she shook her head.

"My food is good. I take care of my children. I always have. Boys don't get fevers for no reason. It just doesn't happen."

We were having breakfast of grits and ham cooked with collard greens, which were bitter and smelled like oil. I pushed them around on my plate. I had been eating collard greens for a week, because Betty insisted they give strength, good blood, long life.

"Flynn Junior ate greens for sixteen years. He grew up big as his daddy. Handsome, too. A big, gorgeous man, L.P.," Betty chastised. "You're going to be just as fine when I get through with you."

I had never thought of myself growing into a big, gorgeous man. Georgia told me I would grow up short to medium height. She said that was fine. Georgia believed shorter men accumulated more money, did more with their careers. Tall men like Violet's new husband Bob loped through life and died poor.

"Eat your greens. No fussing." Betty poured the rest of the coffee into the sink.

I blanched and swallowed. Betty turned to me and crossed her arms.

"I'm driving you over to Carmelita's house today to play with her boy. Make sure your shirt is clean."

"Who's Carmelita?" I asked.

Betty grinned and made a face.

"She's a Mexican woman, L.P., who married a black man. Something I don't approve of. You got to stick with your own kind. It's God's law. But she's a nice gal, a good church woman, even if she's Catholic. Good cook, too."

I brought my plate to the sink and washed it, then put it on a plastic tray to dry, hesitating, waiting in silence. I could feel her thinking. Heat pulsed through the kitchen window. It already had a liquid amber tint, like smoking olive oil, sitting in a forgotten pan.

"They got money, too." Betty tapped her nails on the table. She was speaking to me, but she was also speaking to herself.

"Carmelita was damn lucky if you ask me. She married the only loaded Negro man in Phoenix." Betty looked toward me.

"He's Frank's boss, so you be on your best behavior."

"Are Grover and Samuel coming too?" I asked.

"Yes, yes. It's all been arranged." Betty seemed exhausted. I felt like an expensive doll she might look at, through a store window, something to add to a collection, but the cost made her tired.

I didn't know the name of Carmelita's son until we pulled in the driveway of the only two-story house in South Phoenix that wasn't a church or a business. It was Spanish, with willow trees and a circular driveway. Every window had wrought-iron bars in fancy patterns. I liked the house. It was completely immersed in shade from the delicate willows, and the breeze blew a lacy pattern across its walls.

Grover and Samuel were waving at me. Behind them, a full head taller, was a handsome, cream-colored boy with a black mustache and large, oval brown eyes. I imagined he would grow up wearing white cotton and straw hats. As a man, he would walk in fine white linen suits, know many criminals and dazzle older women. I wasn't sure if I liked him, and I always knew I liked someone on sight or not. It was already a developed trait and one I was proud of.

His mother was standing in the doorway. She was fat and quite short, just a little taller than me. I knew this was Carmelita. She looked like a mother. Immersed in a turquoise silk caftan, she wore turquoise Indian squash blossoms around her neck, three of them, and they were bigger than any I had ever seen. On both wrists, like cuffs, were enormous turquoise bracelets with matching rings. Her earrings were so large they pulled her earlobes down. She held a strand of black beads and a tiny cross. I thought she must make a lot of noise when she walked.

Introductions were made. I had to shake hands, a gesture I was uncomfortable with, as Violet always told me my handshake was weak. That men with strong, firm hands and handshakes were on the level. Men with weak handshakes couldn't be trusted.

Betty stepped forward, the shadows of willows running over her face. Her eyes were foggy under her yellow cotton slip-on turban, a gift from my grandmother, and she was smiling too much.

"L.P., this is my dear friend, Carmelita." I stepped forward and shook Carmelita's hand. Carmelita smiled and I saw three gold teeth. She watched me look at her teeth and smiled even wider, to show them off. All her teeth were capped in gold. I realized she must be very proud of her mouth full of gold.

Carmelita spoke rapidly in Spanish to me. I understood pieces of what she said. Beautiful boy. An honor. Fine family and fine blood.

"Yes, dear, that's right," Betty said, nodding her head. Betty didn't understand a word, and quickly guided me over to the handsome boy. He extended his hand and I took it. He rubbed his thumb on my palm and made me feel funny. No one had ever done this before, and I wondered if it was another language. A code, something secret. I looked at Grover and Samuel to see if they saw, but they weren't paying attention. The boy with the thin mustache continued to rub my palm. Suddenly, Carmelita slapped his hand away. He blushed.

"I'm Davis. Hi, L.P." He stared at me. I could feel the blood in my legs rush to my private parts and it embarrassed me. It was the same feeling I got when things frightened me, or excited me without warning, like when I saw a man take his shirt off at a gas station, then turn away and unzip his trousers, peeing against the wall. I could see hair on the small of his muscled back and a tattoo of a naked woman. I sat straight up and shook my legs until the sensation went away.

I knew this was the Davis that the boys had spoken of in the eucalyptus groves, that probably I would be doing something I had never done before. New, older games. I couldn't understand why Davis wanted to play with Grover, Samuel, and me. Thoughts came and went with the precision of a disaster. He already had a little mustache. He was older. Fifteen. I sensed that if he liked Samuel and Grover, then he must be like me, and I desperately tried to reason, as he took his hand away, what being like me was.

He didn't sound Mexican or black. He sounded like the smartest boy in school, the one who always speaks quietly but firm because he knows he's right. I knew boys like that could get you to do anything they said because you didn't want to look stupid.

Carmelita led us in for lunch in their dining room. It was large and old and dark, with tiled floors and drawn drapes, so during the day the black wrought iron chandelier was on. Our chairs were high, carved, and covered in red velvet deeper than blood. I had seen Tyrone

Power eat in a chair like this, in *Captain from Castile*.
He had leaned back, put his shiny black boots on the
table, laughed and ate a rack of lamb at the same time.
I didn't dare.

Carmelita made us tacos and tamales and she and Betty
talked in quiet, gossipy tones at the far end of the table,
which sat eighteen. Grover, Samuel, Davis, and I sat in
the corner at the far end. Samuel spoke first.

"This place is really neat." Samuel ate a tiny yellow
chile and it burned his mouth. He began drinking all
our water, then had to drink out of the pitcher. Carmelita and Betty didn't notice. We heard low laughter
coming from their end. I wondered how they
communicated.

"Betty says you're rich. Richer than us." It was Davis'
smooth voice. I didn't like the way he said it.

"That's right." I stared at him. I knew I was special.

"What do you like to do, L.P.?" Davis licked his
mustache and I watched, fascinated.

"I like to read and write and I like to climb. I like
colors," I volunteered. I knew I sounded stupid. That I
wasn't getting what he said.

"Samuel kissed L.P. two weeks ago and we didn't
have any clothes on," Grover blurted out, in a conspira-
torial voice. I became frightened. The blood in my legs
started again and I squirmed in my chair.

Grover continued in a whisper. I couldn't tell if he
was telling our secrets because he was frightened of Davis
and wanted to score points, or if he was in awe of
Davis, or maybe Grover was just mean. Maybe he wasn't
my friend.

"L.P. made us promise not to tell anyone, but I knew it was okay to tell you," he said to Davis, who touched his napkin lightly to his upper lip and mustache as he ate the last of Carmelita's tamales.

The way he looked at me made me want to kiss him the way women kiss men in movies, letting their upper shoulders go soft and falling onto the man's chest, their faces tilted upward to catch light, their mouths half open. I wanted to fall into Davis, but I didn't want to know him, or be friends.

Davis talked to Grover and Samuel, deliberately ignoring me, and I studied him closely. His lower lip looked like a sliced cling peach in syrup, still floating at the bottom of the can. His eyes were alert and large and light brown, with thick lashes that were as black as his hair. His shirt was open and his chest was tan; I could see a tiny patch of hair on his chest and I sensed he was an adult but still like me, with a child's hands and eyes. I was still hairless, and the whispering about it at school made it sound like it was still a long time away, two or three years. In a summer that stopped and wrote its own Bible, this was eternity.

Finished with my lunch and knowing I was being watched, I got up and walked like a model over to the barred window. Their backyard was very large and seemed to dip into itself, with rows of grapefruit trees, their trunks painted white to guard against large bugs with glassine shells that bit branches and died there. Carmelita had brought plants from Mexico. I noticed they were in immense terra cotta pots that had turned white with crust and water. I saw floppy monstera vines on redwood lattices that had begun to crumble from heat, and deep green guanacaste trees, the same rank shade as the wishing pond at church. Carmelita had planted poro-poros, with yellow flowers hiding orange flames the tint of traffic lights and memorized suns. I wanted to go out and run through the orchard, count the Mexican flowers by name for my diary. I wanted to bathe in this hot shade and fantasize a movie plot under the grapefruit trees. It seemed like the only thing to do, to get away from the other boys, but I knew I was a guest, that I would have to do whatever was planned.

As Betty blew me a kiss, pointing to her watch and mouthing the words *four P.M.*, I turned to see Davis standing right behind me. Carmelita had vanished, her silver clanking, into the kitchen. As soon as his mother had left, Davis walked up to me and began to kiss me. He stuck his tongue in my mouth as the other boys watched. I struggled, but he was much bigger than I was. His tongue felt like a sea animal in my mouth, and it frightened me.

"Now I've kissed L.P., too." He said this as he pulled away, then wiped his mouth as though my saliva was dirty.

I stood watching the floor, trembling. I did not know whether I liked this or not.

"Let's go outside and play," I said weakly, clearing my throat. I knew I could run outside, and run fast.

"No," Davis hissed. "We're going down to the base-ment. We got a pool table and television and I got magazines. Dirty magazines." Samuel giggled. Davis put his arm around my shoulder like I was a little brother.

I wondered if he had any little brothers, and if he kissed them goodnight, slipping his tongue into their unappreciative mouths. If this was what adults do, it must get messy and wet after a while.

I knew I was going to be the object of ridicule this afternoon and I quickly planned to make myself invisible as possible. To defer plans and fun to the others, to hope they would get caught up in their own dreams and laughter, however cruel, and forget about me. It had worked before.

We walked down stone stairs to the basement, and I thought of Boris Karloff and Bela Lugosi, stone stairs with cobwebs and women with white lace gowns with tattered trains who were damned to be vampires and zombies on strange islands.

When Davis turned on the light in the basement, it was hardly a dungeon. There was avocado green carpeting and space-age furniture with gold nylon upholstery. I saw a pool table, a kidney-shaped, tufted leather bar with electric lanterns and drunks whose noses lit up. With Davis' father being a mortician, I expected coffins.

Grover raced over to the television and turned it on.

"Look, L.P., it's color!" He blurted, running his hands over the screen. I watched, amazed. We still had black-and-white televisions. Georgia thought color TVs were a waste of time and money.

Davis walked over and turned the television off, grinning at the three of us. Grover's face fell into a trance. Samuel tried to whisper to me, but I pushed him away. His breath stank of chiles.

"I got a key to the bar." Davis said this with a smirk.

"I want whiskey," Grover chirped. "My mother drinks whiskey and it makes her laugh."

Davis bent down in back of the bar and opened it. As he got up he looked at his watch. I envied him. I didn't have a watch. He looked so right glancing at his watch. I wondered if he was able to plan bad things because he could keep time.

"This is a secret. Anyone tells we drank whiskey I'll beat you up." Davis meant what he said, and the three of us nodded our heads and crossed our hearts.

"We have to drink it out of the bottle because my dad looks at glasses to see if they're dirty." Davis opened a bottle of Canadian Club. As Grover, Samuel, and I approached the bar, I could smell it.

Davis handed the bottle to Grover. He took a long gulp and choked, then laughed, handing it to Samuel, who began to sip.

"No! Not like that!" Davis yelled. He grabbed the bottle and poured it into his wet mouth, then wiped his lips.

"You got to swallow it fast, otherwise you'll smell like whiskey," Davis said.

Samuel tried again, and managed. The bottle was handed to me. I took a long gulp. I handed it back, trying to look like a secret agent.

"Now I fill it with a little bit of water and no one knows." Davis winked, and I thought him smart.

My heart began beating faster and I could feel the pulse in the back of my neck. I wondered if this is what women felt when they saw a man they liked. I didn't like Davis, but he was showing me already how to do things like a man. And he kept staring at me. Smiling.

Within moments everything got warm. This was different than the beer Betty gave me, which made me pee and sweat. Grover sat on the floor and began to giggle. Samuel began to dance. He reminded me of a marionette.

"I can twist." Samuel puffed, desperately trying his best to twist. We began to laugh. I watched Davis go to another part of the basement and then come back with an armload of magazines.

He said nothing, only tossing the magazines on the floor in front of us. Grover held his breath, then grabbed one. This is what he heard about. Davis' dirty magazines, Davis' games, Davis' basement.

"Look! *Playboy*! And *Stag*!" It was the same voice Grover used when he saw a dead cat in the eucalyptus grove. Grover gingerly began to look through each magazine, stopping at nude photos and grinning, Samuel peering over his shoulder.

I wondered what it was like to be a Playboy Bunny and pose naked on satin sheets with my hair neatly combed. I liked their glossy pink lipstick and the way they didn't smile too much. But the pictures didn't excite me, and I couldn't see what the big deal was. Some nipples were brown and large and some were pink and hard, with little knobs on them. The girls liked to squeeze them so they popped out like two eyes at the camera. I wondered if my mother practiced this in the mirror, and if it was something all women do.

We spent an hour silently handing the magazines back

and forth like scientists, studying each fold-out and full color nude. In *Stag* there were girls in black lace bras

and panties, wearing stiletto heels, holding a gun and looking wild, like they were going to kill. Near each girl was a muscular man with a T-shirt or his shirt off, ready to slap her around. I assumed men found women with guns and messed-up hair very exciting, and that this was one way babies were conceived.

Samuel spoke and cut through the heavy quiet.

"I've got a stiffie."

"Good," said Davis, watching me and Grover. "I've got more magazines." Davis had been sitting next to me with his hand on my knee, which I kept jerking away.

I suddenly thought about Carmelita. If she knew about her son, and why we were so quiet in the basement. If she was relieved for the quiet, going over each black bead with her thumb and forefinger, until she reached her crucifix, then back again, the heavy silver around her neck causing her back to droop, her hunched body serene in the moving, scattering fabric of her willow's shade.

No wonder Betty liked it here, I surmised. It was a closed, cool place. Turning my attention back to Samuel and Grover and Davis, I realized my wrists were limp. I tried to straighten them out.

"How come the hair on her pussy is brown and her hair is blond?" Grover asked, running his hand over the fold-out.

"Because she's not a real blonde," Davis said from the other side of the room. I hadn't realized he had gotten up. He was carrying another bundle of magazines and dropped them on the floor.

"These are real dirty. They show fucking." Davis sat down next to me, then handed Grover and Samuel one called *Bad Girls at Black Rock*. Then he opened one for me.

"L.P. will like this." He said this very soft, like a friend, and I looked inside. There were muscular men dressed in sailor suits with bell bottoms. They were having beers in a bar. As I turned the pages they began to take their clothes off. I had never seen bodies so very muscular, or so perfectly happy at being naked. For me, being naked was an in between part of life, going from one set of clothes to the next. Clothes were much more interesting than being naked, because clothes held fantasy. If I turned a collar up, I was someone else. If I put my mother's dress on when no one was home, I was a queen, or a famous actress.

The men had large penises with curly hair under their arms and on their privates. They played with each other and soon their penises were hard, poking out. I turned the pages faster. Soon one man had his mouth on the other's penis and was swallowing it. There were many pages of him doing this, in different positions. They were happy. Everyone was smiling in this black-and-white world.

"Keep going," Davis urgently whispered to me, "they show everything."

At the last pages the men had a funny expression on their faces. Their mouths were half open and their eyes were looking at the ceiling. They almost looked like they were in pain. White goo was coming out of their penises. I closed the magazine. My forehead was hot, and I realized I was stiff in my pants. My heart was beating so hard I could hear it.

Davis stood up and took his shirt off, then turned to Grover, Samuel, and me.

"I'm going to do a strip tease," Davis said calmly.

Grover looked at Samuel, then at me, and wiped his forehead. Davis went over to a hi-fi that only played forty-fives. He put on "What a Difference a Day Makes" by Dinah Washington. I knew this because I heard Betty play it late at night, when she couldn't sleep.

Davis began to grind his hips, paying no attention to us, humming the lyrics. He took a table lamp and put it on the floor so it could be a spotlight for him, and he began to dance, taking off his polyester slacks, then his socks and shoes, without bending down. He had done this before. He didn't seem to notice us. He put his hands over his underwear and began to rub himself.

I looked over at Grover and Samuel. They were watching in horrified silence, as if they realized too late this was not for them, or me, and that climbing trees was better. But we had to watch. Davis made sure of it. Davis let us see the hair under his arms, which was already thick and black, and a tiny patch of hair on his chest. This was what fathers and boyfriends had, not us. This was three summers away. This was a terror.

Davis was stiff in his underwear. The record turned itself over to a flip side and the new song was very slow, with saxophones. Gradually Davis stood in front of me and peeled his underwear down, then threw it in my face. I froze. There was no light in this basement suddenly, no air, and the only thing was Davis' erect penis waving in front of me, with hair and balls and a hole.

"Kiss it." Davis half spoke. His breath was hard.

"No," I said, moving back on my knees. Davis turned, his penis swinging in the air, and faced Samuel.

"Kiss it," Davis repeated. Samuel looked up at Davis, then at me and Grover, and quietly put his mouth over it. Davis took his hands and pushed Samuel's mouth down on it and Samuel gagged.

Grover giggled. Samuel began to cry. Davis began to pump Samuel's mouth until Samuel broke away and sat down on the floor, weeping. As soon as he did, Davis pulled on his penis and that same white fluid spurted out. We were silent as Davis groaned. His semen hit the pages of the magazines. When he was finished, he quickly bent over and hurriedly closed the magazines like a child, as if by closing them his imaginary gods were put away. Grover put his arm around Samuel and motioned for me to come over. As I did, I saw Davis become very feminine, tsking and straightening up his magazines, which he quickly took back to their hiding places. He was like me, I knew it, but I felt sorry for him. He was sad, not powerful. He wasn't an enemy or a friend, only someone to forget.

"It's okay. It's okay." Grover took a monogrammed handkerchief and gave it to Samuel, who blew his nose.

"It tasted like salt," Samuel murmured to himself. "I hate it."

Davis' voice slithered through the distance of the basement.

"You tell anybody and I'll kill you. You'll be a dead body in my father's morgue and I'll pee all over you."

Davis looked like the fighters I'd seen on the news. I watched his penis swing back and up, like it couldn't decide what to do.

Samuel continued to sob. Grover seemed depressed. Some basement party. Davis didn't stop staring at me, and my face flushed.

I heard Carmelita rushing upstairs. Her jewelry preceded her.

"Put your clothes on. I hear your mom," I said quickly. Davis grinned at me, thinking me a conspirator and a friend. I was neither. I knew acting would make everything run smooth.

"That was really neat, Davis," I said, staring at Grover and Samuel, trying to explain to them silently it was time to go, but play along.

Davis' large brown eyes squinted as he bent down to pick up the table lamp. His face suddenly became drawn and cruel.

"Remember. Anyone of you tell and you'll be dead bodies and I'll eat your eyeballs and rip out your guts." Suddenly he smiled.

"I got a girlfriend." Davis said this like a lie.

"Boy, is she lucky." I said this in a high-pitched voice, and swallowed, but my mouth was dry.

I heard Carmelita at the stairs. I was surprised Davis didn't hear her.

"Turn on the TV quick," I murmured, "*The Addams Family* is on channel five."

When Carmelita came down with cookies and milk,

we were sitting in front of the television, snapping our fingers to the theme song of *The Addams Family*. She smiled, smelled the room, and looked at us with distrust. Carmelita laid the cookies down and walked with slow, heavy steps back up the stairs.

"I like you, L.P. I want you to come back and play," Davis said, licking his lips.

"Sure," I said, watching Grover and Samuel. "It was fun, Davis."

In Betty's car, Grover and Samuel and I said nothing. We were sweating in the early August afternoon, and I knew Grover and Samuel would have to go back to see Davis, that their parents thought they were friends. I didn't have to. I was the outsider, the guest from a finer, whiter world, and I was only looking in. I forgot Davis as I forgot anything without the satisfaction of kindness and color. But I dreamed of Carmelita, two nights later.

She held a crucifix and there were poro-poros in her hair. Her head looked like it was on fire and she was waving to me from her front door, holding up the crucifix to ward away vampires. Davis ran naked under the willows, laughing in a scream, and the faster he ran, the more Carmelita's head burned. She called for Dios and the Sacred Virgin. Davis ran until he was a blur and the house was covered in dust. I wonder if, like Sambo, he turned into butter.

Dropping Grover and Samuel off, I waved to them, but they didn't wave back. I saw the backs of their heads disappear into the front doors of concrete bungalows with lawns and rotating sprinklers. Marcelline came out and waved to Betty at Grover's house. She was dressed in a housedress of purple flowers and had curlers in her hair. At Samuel's, Lucille came out, putting her horn-rim glasses away and taking out another pair of prescription sunglasses, saw us, then waved. She was holding a can of tomato sauce in her hand.

There was no wind, and I realized some women move in a painting. They are forever framed against a much prettier sky, and their lives are small, but they try. I would try for the rest of this summer to frame myself against that desert sky, then step outside and try to look in, but I couldn't. I would try to draw myself climbing eucalyptus trees and see my silhouette in a noonday sun, but my pencil wouldn't work. I tried crayons from a thick package that had every color, but the blues were too pure, the yellows insufficient to grasp what it was to forget, then remember.

My mother would be home soon and she loved me, even if she was married. My grandmother would be home soon and she promised me everything rich and fine in the world.

Samuel and Grover would never leave Phoenix. A backseat voice told me this, with Betty chatting in the front. Samuel and Grover would have families and forget me as fast as I forgot them, perhaps.

We had been hurt, but we didn't know it. Like the casual, planned language of a cruel adult, it made us think, not cry. It made us thankful for shadows. It made me realize I could count a bruise for every afternoon I lived, like a sunset, like Betty's blood of the sun.

But I hadn't fallen, been beaten, or drawn blood. I had watched, because I had to, a teenage boy masturbate, something my penis as yet could not do, and I knew this was natural. I admitted to myself I liked the aroma of young men, the way semen smelled of earth and sea-water. And I knew, after this summer, that I could talk my way out of any danger. Always.

Secretly I tried to decide if the hair on my body would look like Davis', when I got to his age, or maybe I would be a blond, like Anita Ekberg. I knew I wanted to be smooth. Perfect.

Davis would kill someone purely for pleasure. I could smell it on his skin and I shuddered. But Betty was here with me now, and Frank would be home for dinner and television, and I would lay on my bed on the back porch and watch light evaporate, methodically deciding what to count, what to remember, and what to forget.

THE NEXT DAY I decided to go to Samuel's house to see if he wanted to play by the canal. Crisp desert weeds the color of postal wrapping paper had grown even higher since our last visit. I wanted to play with Samuel like Joan Collins in *Empire of the Ants,* where she hacked her way through a jungle, all for the love of one man. And wore dark red lipstick as she fought off hordes of huge army ants.

Samuel lived only two blocks from Betty. It was the exact same house, low slung and all concrete, but Lucille had painted the house a Caribbean yellow and took great pains to plant banana trees around the front door, all of which died. They looked scary at night, all shriveled and pointing to me under the desert moon. One night in July Betty had dropped Samuel off at that strange yellow bungalow, and I whispered to him to keep an eye on those banana trees. He nodded his head. He knew.

I had to walk on lawns because I was barefoot and the streets were boiling, easily tearing a layer of skin off the bottoms of my feet. I took off my shoes, a pair of red sneakers, not one door away from Betty's. I wanted to be barefoot all day, walking through vacant lots and flower fields.

I walked through sprinklers and my clothes were soaked. They dried quickly, and it didn't matter. I was Lawrence of Arabia.

At Samuel's front door I heard Samuel scream. The screen door was locked, or I would have run in. Lucille was yelling in the background. The radio was on, and Diana Ross and the Supremes were singing "I Hear a Symphony." I heard somebody bump against a wall. A whimper, then Lucille screaming.

It was a sad, tiny kind of bump. I was reminded how, sometimes, in the middle of the night, the night birds in Betty's backyard would fly against the dark screen of my porch, then drop, stunned. Singing in the dark trees would cease until that one bird picked itself up, its wings suddenly spastic and heavy. First it had to fly back to the dark trees. Then the songs would begin again. I realized the smallest of sounds can be the ones causing the most intense pain.

"You're not right in the head, you little nigger bastard. Stand up when I'm talking to you. What are you, a dog? Get up, stop walking on all fours, and Christ, stop crying."

I could see Lucille's back; the rest of her was in another room. I saw a vague shadow of someone small trying to right himself, trying to stand up straight.

I hoped, at that moment, that God said a special prayer for everyone that was small. And helpless, those of us who got knocked down. Those of us who were trying to survive, adapt, love. I wondered if God prayed too.

"Oh Christ, tie your fucking shoelaces and zip up your zipper. No one wants to see your little dangle, lease of all me. Fucking little nigger know-it-all. You can't even tie your own shoelaces."

A chill swept my cheeks and shoulders. My eyes were tearing and I wiped off their wetness just as Lucille appeared from behind the screen, the veins in her neck pulsing, and her eyes cruel, darting all over me.

"What the hell do you want, white boy? You want to play with Samuel? Well, honey, Samuel's a dog, he doesn't know how to stand up like a man. He's a dog like his pappy, a bastard. You got that, white boy? You wanna play with a dog? Here he is."

"I'm here! I'm here, L.P." It was Samuel's voice, soft but strong, coming from the shadows. I saw his face appear through the blackened netting. His right eye was swollen.

"What a shiner," I said aloud. I had heard Clark Gable say that when he looked in the mirror in an old movie. Then he sort of smiled with a smirk.

"He's clumsy, L.P. He tripped." Lucille turned away from us briefly to go to her smoked-mirror coffee table and light a cigarette. She turned back to Samuel and me. Lucille twitched suddenly and put on her horn-rim glasses.

"I got lots of money. Betty gave Samuel and me money for hamburgers and fried shrimp. Can Samuel come out?" I asked sweetly.

Samuel turned hesitantly to his mother.

"Please, Mama." His voice was quiet, but it sounded as though he understood why his mother was mean.

Lucille paused with her cigarette. Where Betty's bungalow was a dark, welcoming purple, Lucille's house was as bright inside as its paint outside. All the lights in the living room were on and, from what I could see, the rest of the house was dark, with closed curtains.

"Please. Betty thought we'd have fun," I said in a slight whine.

Lucille flicked her nails, the ash from her cigarette going all over her rust-colored carpet. She managed a tight, ripe smile and murmured a yes.

"If Betty said yes . . ."

Within a few seconds Samuel was outside, the screen door banging in back of him. He had bruises on his knee and his arm. He limped. There was blood on his elbows and knees.

"You're limping," I said, astonished.

"I'll be okay, L.P. Let's just walk, okay?" Samuel was in control, I knew it. Even though he was limping, he was walking very fast, and I had to hop on my bare feet to keep up with him.

"Let's just keep walking, L.P. Far, far away." Samuel was crying as he limped toward our canal, but he stared right ahead, like a racehorse or a greyhound, like any

animal with blinders and a bit, living in a cage, waiting
to run again.

"What happened?" I asked, almost out of breath.

Samuel stopped for a moment, and blew his nose in
his pocket handkerchief.

"You're a gentleman," I said brightly. "You use a
hanky. Like Grover."

Samuel began to cry. He looked at me and dropped
his handkerchief. I watched him begin to shake, his arms
numb at his sides. He kept moaning and I walked over
to Samuel and touched his face with my hand.

"We're here, Samuel. We're in the tall grasses, by the
river, and the great trees are just over there. You don't
have to cry now."

I bent over and picked up his handkerchief and put
it in his hand. Samuel wasn't crying as hard, but he was
still shaking, and his sobs sounded like hiccups.

A wind came up as though an oven door had been
opened. The tall grasses around us began to clatter and
shimmy and I knew Samuel and I should sit in the shade.
I put my arms around him suddenly. It felt right to me.
Samuel kept crying, and bent my head towards him, and
I kissed him. And then he kissed me back. We looked
at each other for a long time in the sun, kissed once
more and made it long like in the movies, then walked
to the shade of the swaying eucalyptus trees.

I had lied to Lucille. Betty hadn't given me money
for hamburgers and fried shrimp. She didn't even know
I was out in a hundred and five degree weather. Samuel
needed to be rescued, I decided to myself.

We found a shady place where the high weeds had already been trampled on and I thought it was very pretty, like a grass bed with the sun dappled and the tree's shade moving in the wind.

Samuel lay down with some difficulty. He was shaky in his knees and wrists. I quickly lay down next to him and put my arms around his stomach, leaning my head on his small shoulder.

"Look up at the sky," I said quietly.

I watched Samuel's eyes become clear, pensive. We listened to the dry grasses.

"Think there are snakes?" Samuel suddenly asked.

"No. Besides, I like snakes. I don't like spiders though," I said, disturbed by this. "I love to look at the sky, Samuel. Look how big it is. Is it white or is it blue?"

"It's a white man's world. So I guess it's white," Samuel whispered. I kissed him again, simply because I wanted to. It felt good, and Samuel didn't mind at all. The eucalyptus tree over us was sending down a fluffy pollen.

"What was it like, Samuel? What did it taste like?" I asked in a low voice.

Samuel thought for a moment.

"I don't know. Kind of big and salty, and it smelled like the ocean. I liked it when it first went in, but he made me gag."

"Did you like it?" I asked gently.

"Yes." Samuel looked into my eyes. "You were watching. You liked it, too."

I nodded my head.

"Why does it make me feel funny?" I thought to

myself, murmuring it on my lips as the wind passed over us. Samuel craned his head over and kissed me again. This time he put his tongue on mine. I let him. His skin was a beautiful brown, like leather sofas and wet desert dirt, and I liked what I felt. When we finished kissing I rubbed the top of his head.

"I like your hair," I said quite seriously. "The curls are so small."

"There's not much of it," Samuel said with a sigh. "Mama won't let me wear it anything but short."

"Your mama beat you up, didn't she?" I asked in his ear.

Samuel was about to say something, but he stopped, and looked up at the sky. His right eye was big as a plum.

"It hurts. It hurts all over." Samuel stared up, not at me.

"I know it does," I said quietly. I decided to somehow discuss pleasant matters. I had watched my grandmother and mother practice this avoidance with an expert flair. There would be a collective sigh between the two, then the smiles would begin, the voices buoyant.

"L.P., what are you going to be when you grow up?"

"I'm going to be a movie star, like Sophia Loren, and live in Rome and eat spaghetti every day and wear lots of makeup," I said with conviction.

Samuel laughed. "No. Who are you going to be?"

I stared at Samuel.

"I like boys, I think," I said reasonably. "Who do you like?"

Samuel paused. There was mucus on his nose from the crying and I made him clean it off with his hanky.

"I like boys, too, L.P. Are they going to kill us because we kissed?"

"Not if you don't tell." I thought about Samuel and myself. Maybe we were the only boys who liked other boys, but I remembered the magazines in Davis' basement, and realized they made actual magazines for boys like us. A lot of us must be in the adult world. We must have our own, separate country somewhere.

"My mama told me she knows, and that's why she hates me. What did I do? I didn't do anything to her."

I nodded my head.

"My mama hates me, too." When I heard my own words I stopped playing with Samuel's hair.

"Is that why you live with Betty now, L.P.?" Samuel's voice was innocent.

"No. I'm staying with Betty for the summer, that's all. My mama got married and she's on her honeymoon."

"For three months?" Samuel's voice was incredulous. I became angry with him.

"I don't want to talk about it," I said into the wind. I tried to sit up, but Samuel pulled me back down to him. I looked at his swollen eye and I could feel tears in mine. He looked at me and touched my eyes, rubbing the tears between his fingers.

"I stopped crying, L.P. Now you'll have to."

"Does this mean I'm not allowed to kiss you, or cry, or hold you? I don't understand. Why is this so bad? Why do people hate us?"

"My mama says I'm not natural, L.P. So that means you're not natural, too."

"Does this mean we're like Dracula's daughter?" I asked.

"Yes."

"I want to go away from here and never come back, ever. Samuel, will you go with me, never leave me?"

Samuel kissed me again.

"You're a white boy," was all he said.

Samuel limped slowly home with me. I even put on my shoes. We both had to squint, as the sun throbbed and danced above us. I told Samuel to look at the ground, it was easier, not so hard on the eyes.

"I thought you wanted me to look up at the sky, L.P.," Samuel said. His lips were chapped, and he was breathing strangely as he limped.

"Oh, that too. You have to look all over the place." We both laughed. Then we decided to play the where-am-I-now game.

"Right now I'm in New York City on the top of the Empire State Building drinking champagne," I said with excitement.

"Right now I'm in Hollywood and there are a lot of cameras. And I'm blond. And I'm naked," I said with a growing sense of wonder.

"Right now I'm naked, too, and you're still blond, and we're both in bed, like a man and a woman, and I'm on top of you like the man does." Samuel tittered.

"See, we can be anyone we want," I said smugly.

As we neared Samuel's house he grabbed my arm.

"L.P., you fly away. Soon as I can, I'm going, too. I'm scared. I don't want to be alone and we're alone. I won't know who to talk to."

"Talk to me."

"You'll be gone. You'll be alone, too."

Yes, Samuel, I thought, I will be alone all my life. I had gotten used to being alone, invisible as a breeze. I wasn't lonely, and I wasn't afraid.

Aisha was sitting on a beer keg by Samuel's front door. She was wearing large hoops with red balls on her ears, and gold stars, the kind I got at school, on the glittered, upper lids of her eyes.

Samuel faced me and smiled.

"I really like you, L.P."

"I like you, too, Samuel."

We didn't hug or kiss because Aisha was watching, but I don't think she would have minded.

"See, L.P., my mama's sick. She's got nervous problems. She's just sick." Samuel's eyes became sad, resigned. I didn't understand his fate, and I wanted to, desperately. As he turned around, Aisha stood up and walked out into the sunlight. The glitter and stars on her eyelids sparkled, but her eyes were livid, destroyed.

Slowly Samuel limped through the front yard toward his big sister. Samuel was smiling, but at this point I think he could only see out of one eye. He moved with the exhausted grace of a soldier returning home. I thought he was beautiful.

"Oh baby, little baby boy." Aisha clutched Samuel, then let out a scream of rage. "Who did this to you? Who? Did that bitch do this to you?"

I saw Samuel murmur as if offering an apology, then shake his head. Aisha glared at me, motioning for me to go. She covered his swollen face with her hands, which had silver rings on every finger, and she began to cry.

"Go away, white boy. L.P., go away and don't you say nothing, you hear? You just go and head on home now." Aisha cleared her throat and stared at me.

"Please."

I had never heard a voice come from the gut the way Aisha's did. It was as though an older woman was down inside her, clawing her way out.

I cocked my head and tried to smile, to let her know it was okay. I couldn't turn away, I had to keep my eyes on Samuel because I loved him. I loved the way his lips kissed, and his hair, I loved the way he let me put my arms around him, the way he whispered in my ear.

I backed away in small steps, watching Aisha scream and run into the house. Suddenly the sound of two female voices, uttering oaths and hatred and threats, and I knew where I was. Suddenly the sound of china being broken, glasses shattered, a hysteria blooming on a hot summer afternoon like a magnolia flower, opening big and mean on the tree, then turning to brown in the sun.

Samuel opened the screen door and walked inside, letting it slam behind him. Next door the neighbors had come out to turn their sprinklers off, and barely paid any attention to the noises coming from Lucille's living room. The sky was white, just as Samuel had said. As I continued to step backwards, I saw his face behind the netting. He looked at me, and kissed the screen.

{*fifteen*}

"BETTY, WHY HASN'T Mama sent me a postcard?"

It was the middle of August. 3 P.M. An informality
had been born between us. I no longer asked to play with
Grover and Samuel, and Betty didn't press me. With the
head, it was easier to stay inside, go to a movie, eat late
at night, when the kitchen was cool. I had moved my
television watching from the back porch to the living
room when Frank wasn't home, and positioned an electric fan near the sofa. Betty's air-conditioning unit had
to be put on low or it would blow a fuse.

"Honey, your mama has a man. She's in love. She'll
be back."

Betty was watching *General Hospital* with me, eating
unshelled peanuts from a large plastic bag. She had an
African caftan on.

I loved her living room now, and understood its purple shadows. I could fall into a warm sleep in the middle of the afternoon and wake to a persistence of lavenders and the sense that nothing changes. These shadows were secure. No one could touch us here. The sun could bleach and cook and make us sick. I decided my mother knew I would be safe in this purple resting place, that everything would stay clean around me, and cool.

Betty was tired of snapping peanuts shells, and she switched the television off.

"Nothing's going on today. Doctor Prentiss isn't going to help Emily. Not a bit. It's not fair," she remarked distantly.

Betty rose and dusted her hands off.

"I'll have to vacuum again," she muttered, "but that can wait. What do you say, L.P., to a movie? It's cool in the theaters."

I liked the idea, and got up.

"What's on at the Fox? Let's go there," I announced. I loved the Fox Theater. It was the only movie palace in Phoenix, built in the twenties. The Fox had chandeliers, and marble bathrooms with gold faucets. There was a fresco of the sky, with angels, like Michelangelo's, on the ceiling of the main theater. It was the biggest dark room I'd ever been in, and I always tried to count the angels before the lights went down. There was never enough time.

The Fox had a balcony and special side booths perched high, and regal, with castle turrets and gilt angels. I had tried to find them so I could sit and watch movies from such an exalted position, but the halls leading to them were covered in dust and cordoned off with red velvet ropes.

I loved the way, no matter how loud you were in the theater, no one could hear you. No one went to the Fox anymore, because it was downtown. People went to the Palms on Central Avenue, or the Bethany Theater near Chris Town, on Bethany Home Road. The only people at the Fox were colored people and old, drunk men who sat in the back row, in the shadows. Sometimes I saw them moving, sitting next to each other briefly, then moving on. I wondered what they did. If they played musical chairs in that serious darkness for fun.

The refreshment stand at the Fox had gold columns with leaves and grapes and leaping deer. Their popcorn wasn't good. It came in thin red striped paper bags that broke if you touched them the wrong way. But their candy astonished. There were brands from Mexico with coconut and old-fashioned boxes of chocolates with red bows under a sign that said FOR YOUR SWEETHEART. There were hot dogs, candy corn balls, and cotton candy made fresh from a hot rattling machine that sucked in all the air around it. You could pick your colors and I loved them: hot pink, electric green, aqua, peach, lemon yellow, cherry red.

I wanted my house to look just like the Fox, with chandeliers and ruby-red carpet and stairs that ten people could walk side by side and still have plenty of room. I wanted to be able to turn the corner and see something carved, golden, because God said so, and be able to walk into its cavern and see movies forever. I had memorized

Eastmancolor, Technicolor, CinemaScope, Panavision, Todd-AO, MGM, Twentieth Century-Fox, Paramount Pictures. Their names stuck on my tongue like a chant, rolling beautifully into the air. I wondered how anyone could think up such impressive, pretty words. I loved the lion and the woman holding a torch, the mountain with snow and stars, the earth spinning slowly and silently with a Universal logo. This was my church, a safe magic. All I had to do was sit and watch.

The first film I remember seeing at the Fox was *Cleopatra,* with Elizabeth Taylor and Richard Burton. My mother had taken me to the road show when I was four, almost five. She put her hands over my eyes when Liz bathed in ass' milk. But I remember her entrance to Rome, pulled by hundreds of slaves on a giant Sphinx, and I thought she wouldn't fit into the theater. I ran up the aisles and opened the doors to the lobby so she would have more room. My mother was furious. Elizabeth Taylor was her goddess, as Sophia Loren was mine. They helped us reason the world into simple, glamorous terms. You either looked like them, or did your best to try.

We sat down in the balcony of the Fox for a double feature of Elvis Presley films, even though I didn't like him. I wanted to see Sophia Loren in *Lady L,* but Betty loved Elvis. She left a note on the refrigerator for Frank that we would be home at eight P.M. We had to sit in the balcony because coloreds were frowned upon on the main floor, but I didn't mind. From the balcony I realized you could kill yourself if you jumped, and thought it dangerous and very James Bond. I was able to peer through the sputter of color and light and music into the royal boxes on the side. Elvis was singing about Acapulco and I imagined there were ghosts sitting in the booths, and vampires ready to grab children. I sunk further into my chair, and stared up at the ceiling. The angels here were closer.

Betty was smoking a Kool and a woman with a beehive hairdo, in back of us, told her to put it out. Betty swore under her breath, stubbed the cigarette out with her sandal, and handed me a box of Jordan Almonds.

I watched the movie with disinterest. I was happy to be here and the air-conditioning felt good. I liked one scene where Mexican mariachi men with ruffled polka dot shirts played their maracas. Elvis started singing and suddenly girls in fluorescent bikinis appeared out of nowhere and everyone began to do the Jerk. It was very jet-set and fast.

After Elvis and Acapulco, we started watching the second bill, called *Roustabout,* and Elvis was singing on a carnival ride. Halfway through, a black woman put her hand on Betty's shoulder in the dark, and whispered something in her ear. Betty gasped. She mentioned for me to sit still while she went with this shadow, and she didn't come back for a half an hour.

In that time I turned around and looked at the rest of the balcony. I saw two tired servicemen, one sleeping on the other's shoulder. There was a group of shifting men in the far back row, the one so far up the movie screen looked like a portable television, and they seemed to be playing musical chairs like the men on the ground floor. I wondered if this had something to do with what Davis had showed me. The white semen that made babies. But why in a movie theater? Directly in back of me I saw the black woman with the beehive hairdo that shhed Betty, and she was sitting next to an elderly black woman with a wilted paper flower pillbox hat who was snoring. I assumed it was her mother.

When I turned around, Elvis was singing on top of a hayride and more girls, this time in Li'l Abner bikinis, were doing the Jerk. When I turned around the two Negro ladies had moved to another end of the balcony. They didn't like me turning around so much. It destroyed their concentration. I decided these women came to the movies every day, that they had already seen Elvis sing over two hundred times, and they were miserable, but it was the only cool place that cost fifty cents to get in. Maybe they didn't have a home, and this was the place they ate lunch, breakfast, and dinner, and they washed their hair in the ladies' room, which had French mirrors and large velvet sofas and candelabra lights. I knew, because I had snuck inside once.

When Betty came back to her seat, she pulled me up. I spilled the rest of the Jordan Almonds. I bent down to retrieve the box because there was a contest on the back, and she pulled at me again.

"No, L.P. We've got to go now. Right away. Something bad," Betty whispered.

Her voice had the quality of tin being rained on, and I knew instantly she was crying, but trying to keep her voice down. It didn't matter. No one was listening.

Her hands were desperately leading me down the

grand staircase and her grip hurt. She clutched me so hard I could feel her pulse. Elvis echoed through the lobby and a man with slicked, bouffant hair and a bolo tie was cleaning ashtrays out. He was dancing to the music.

In the light of the lobby I saw Betty's face. Her eyes were red and she was walking without feet, letting her head direct her to the etched glass doors.

"Who was that woman?" It was all I could think of to ask.

Betty swung the doors open without looking at me and talked briskly, typing a memorandum in her head.

"It was Myrna. She's the office secretary here. Someone from the hospital. Someone saw my note on the refrigerator. Myrna knew we were in the balcony. Myrna knew Frank."

Her last sentence frightened me. The light outside was crisp and full of darkening blue. We were walking faster than I was used to, and I panted. I saw Betty's car parked down the street, which was odd, because we had parked it in the parking lot in back.

"What hospital?" I asked.

"All Saints." Betty talked to herself, not letting go of my arm. "Room 1106, on the first floor, toward the rear. I check in with the night nurse. Her name is Josephine. She has forms."

We got in the car. I saw the window of a pet shop, dozens of bird cages with cotton sheets over them. The lights were dimmed in the store. A rattlesnake was making its way down the sidewalk and I screamed.

Betty caught her breath in front of the steering wheel.

She stiffened when I screamed. As though she woke from a sweat. She looked out the window.

"Shut up, L.P. It's a snake. That's all it is," Betty said. Her lower lip began to tremble and Betty began to sob. I heard moans that came from an ancient place. She tried to put the key in the steering wheel ignition. When she couldn't, she began to beat it with her fists.

This was a permanent, wounded moment. It bled with hues and tints of someone dying, of women who can't start cars, their purses spilling cosmetics on the floors, their hands trying to conquer the simple act of steering, making a right turn when the earth is turning to black and will stay that way. Betty had been here before.

"You do it, honey." She handed me the keys.

I stopped shaking, and leaned over, putting the correct key in the ignition. My screaming seemed silly. The rattlesnake slid down the street. Betty started the car.

"Roll down the windows. I need air." Betty snapped her fingers at me. I rolled down my window and stuck my head and one arm out as we began to move. I wanted to feel the impaled, bone smooth wind of this descending summer night. No cars were on the street. This was the time for silence. This was the time when sun and moon faced one another on opposite horizons, a conjunction of locust and streetlights berthing moths, of squalor and solitude. I liked downtown Phoenix when it was empty. When people could drive fast as they wanted to, making echoes, tire marks, and gasoline dust. I knew something terrible had happened. Birds were asleep in their cages and snakes coiled outside the door.

*   *   *

I put my head inside the car because my lips were getting chapped. Betty kept repeating an undecipherable prayer on the edge of her lips. I watched her face pass through shadows and lights. She didn't blink. Her eyes became large, transcendent, her yellow-green pupils darting through their own maze, startled and near incineration.

We passed Indian women who stopped and watched our car heave past. They knew what was happening. I saw them make a signal with their arms like a clap, then expanded to encompass a bird flying. They stepped back on the sidewalk as we drove by. They were praying for Betty.

All Saints Hospital looked like a prison with gardens. The windows had bars built in the glass, and I saw a sign that read SANITORIUM and another sign, CARDIO-VASCULAR. As we got out of the car, we walked toward the sanitorium, and I pulled on Betty's sleeve.

"That's for crazy people." I was terrified.

"L.P., listen." Betty bent down. She ran her hand over my face. "It's the only section that takes colored people. We don't go in the big building. It's okay." Her voice was soothing, tired, immobile.

I stopped walking.

"I'll wait here," I said.

"The hell you will," she said, grabbing my head, then my upper arm.

"Why? What's in there?" I shrieked. The front doors had iron bars on them.

"Goddamit child! Frank had a stroke. He's bad. Real bad." Betty slapped me. I had never been slapped before.

I could feel the air come out of me, an electricity fly with her hand back to her side.

"I'm sorry, L.P.," she said, without conviction. "Please."

"I'm sorry, Betty," I mumbled. The streetlights turned themselves on. I followed her inside.

Inside, I was made to sit on a lawn chair next to Frank's door. Air whisked over me as nurses came in and out. Betty went in, and turned to smile at me. It was hard for her not to cry.

"You be my friend tonight, okay? Whatever I do or say tonight, L.P., you don't pay any attention. You understand?"

I nodded my head. She was gone. Into the room. I could smell antiseptic and something like a drawn, gassy odor, like my grandfather's oxygen tank at home.

A nurse gave me a *Highlights for Children* to read, which I hated. I was way too old for *Highlights for Children*. I kept it in my lap and looked around. The walls of this corridor were a glassy turquoise with Indian sand paintings on board, hanging in chipped frames. The staff here was black and fat, dressed in crisp white that looked like it could draw blood. They laughed and pushed aluminum carts. Some pushed wheelchairs with very old black people whose heads bobbed around. I tried to reason my death.

I wondered if my head would bob around like a water balloon on my shoulders. If I wouldn't understand anything said to me, after trying so hard to be understood. If all I heard was the wheelchair, a door opening to another room where the light was too bright, trying to make sense of turquoise walls and my heartbeat, counting the days until the flutter and jolt stopped.

I decided death had colors. White, burgundy, carmine, sienna, perhaps black. And the longer you stayed dead, the greener the colors became, until it was like a jungle, and then those colors became flesh, and the next thing you knew, you were born again.

Then I considered the possibility of never dying. I knew it was in my hands, that if I prayed hard enough, I could strike a bargain with God. He would listen.

A woman walked by me in a white dressing gown. As she passed by, I saw her strings weren't tied and her rear end had many wrinkles that jiggled as she walked. I giggled and she heard me.

She turned around and smiled at me. She was a white lady. Her teeth were missing and her hair hung around her like dead fish stored on a line. I could see her eyes were blue, that she had tried to put makeup on, but missed, sending the pencil down her cheek.

"You aren't supposed to peek," she said thickly. She spit on the floor. I focused my eyes on my lap. Her voice got louder.

"You aren't supposed to peek!" she wailed. Suddenly, a black nurse with "Hilda" on her nameplate, put her arm around the woman and gently guided her away, down the hall. I could hear the woman sobbing.

"He peeked, Hilda. He saw."

"It's nothing. He's just a little boy." Their voices drifted into a room. The door closed. A telephone rang.

A chill made my knees shake. I didn't want to be here. Someone here could stab me. I knew madness doesn't come on top of a mountain or a tree, or swimming, but here, in rooms where the lights aren't turned off. I closed my eyes and tried to find the spots. They were there, a grisly cream, and shimmering. I opened them again.

Hilda was standing next to me.

"You need to go to the bathroom, honey?"

I shook my head no. Hilda was blue-black and wore a man's watch. But her nails were painted dainty pink, and they were long. I could smell magnolia perfume on her wrists.

"Sweetpea, it gets scary in here when you don't understand. See, they's sick with things. Sometimes it's in their brain, like a bee buzzing inside, and they can't get it out."

"Couldn't it go out through their ears?" I asked. It seemed the only way besides their mouth or nose. Hilda laughed.

"No." She reached in her pocket and handed me a crushed Twinkie.

"I keep them for my favorites. Here. You got a long wait."

God was good to me that night. The hum of the hospital air-conditioning put me to sleep. And I dreamed with sound. Particularly echoes. And waves.

I was at Pacific Beach, near San Diego, at the old amusement park. My mother was with me, pulling me toward the huge old rollercoaster.

"C'mon, it'll be fun," she said. Her eyes were marbles. Her hair reached to the ground.

I could smell seaweed further ahead, at the beach. Giant mountains of kelp lay stranded and slippery near the shore. It was high tide. Ten-foot waves were crashing in my dream. I could smell sea spray. The sun was bright.

I put my hands over my eyes and looked at the waves and the kelp. The kelp was alive, moving as though in a science fiction film. It was absorbing, eating all the children on the beach. I screamed. Then I saw that their parents were laughing, throwing them into the kelp.

"C'mon, L.P., we don't have all day." My mother's arm tugged at me again. I screamed and ran. I ran past plastic ducks, floating in water, hit with rifle BBs, past carnival glass and milk glass and tattoos drawn on paper, fluttering in the heavy sea air. My feet didn't touch the littered pavement and I kept trying to push through my neck, to grow my dragonfly wings, but they wouldn't come.

Then I ran into the arms of a young sailor, his skin like bleached wood, with blue eyes. He laughed, grabbed me and began to kiss me, saying, "I love you, we'll sail far away, you'll be my wife." I let him kiss me, then pushed myself away.

He disappeared. Instead, my mother was once again in front of me, begging me sweetly.

"Please, L.P. Please!"

I didn't know what to do. I took her hand.

The next thing I knew our car on the rollercoaster lurched forward. We began to climb. Up toward the sun. My mother turned to me. She smiled. There was blood on her teeth.

"This is a real scary ride, L.P.," she said in her best singsong voice, "and they say no one comes back. It's the first hill. The tracks aren't connected."

Violet clapped her hands excitedly. We were almost at the top.

"Here . . . we go!" She screamed.

At the top I began to struggle. There weren't any tracks left. Just twisted iron and space. I looked up to the sun and began to cry. A wave broke in the distance. We went off the tracks, down, down. Another wave broke. Then silence.

It was very early in the morning when I woke up. I was curled in the lawn chair. Someone had put an orange blanket that smelled like vomit over me, but I hadn't noticed.

Betty was leaning against the wall, smoking a Kool, watching me. She was utterly still, as though she didn't have blood or water in her body, that she would scatter like a leaf. I saw her face was glazed, smooth.

"Let's go home, L.P. Frank's dead."

I didn't know how to cry for Frank. I thought I should, but he wasn't my father, or grandfather. I liked him. Suddenly tears came streaming onto my shirt.

"You don't have to cry, honey. It's okay." Betty said this in a monotone. "We've got to go back home, L.P. I'm very tired. There's a lot to do. Stand up."

I did as I was told.

At the house Betty moved slowly around, brushing past her furniture and touching it as though she had never seen it before. In the kitchen she made me a sandwich and smiled, sitting across from me with her hands folded in her lap. Her hunch seemed to be painful, and she shifted around crossly. But her face was devoid of any grimace; rather it was sitting, waiting for a pardon I couldn't draw, or count, or reason.

"No one really suffers when their mind is on the next step out," Betty said, breaking the early morning numbness. I finished chewing my sandwich. I knew I didn't have to say anything at all.

Betty hadn't spoken to me, but to herself. She was watching the beginnings of dawn light filter through the kitchen window. I could hear night birds. Betty sipped her coffee, then spoke again.

"Consider all the untruths you have lived with, and ignored." She paused to take a breath, "And you will have every answer you need. They cover something dense and sweet. Like icing on a poison that takes years to go bad."

The night birds called each other in a shrill, tropical opera. As the dawn strengthened and smoothed out their caws, Betty rose and turned the kitchen light off, letting us sit in the shadows. She stood, staring out the window at electric wires and cacti, her cigarette smoke lying in a still shelf of air. There was a light around her I'd seen before, in old women at Catholic Church. They'd bring their lunches with them in the pews, sitting in that distilled light until Midnight Mass. It was the concentration of fanaticism, the ability to sit alone until you believe God touched your shoulder.

We both listened to the cantata, the way those night birds blended notes into what must have been love songs. I thought how this is what flowers would sound like if they sang, tiny rounded notes softened with feathers and impending light. Only their music would be perfumed.

"It's just us, L.P. You're all mine. You're all I've got." I trembled. I thought she wasn't making sense, but she had told me not to pay attention to anything tonight.

"You're my boy, L.P. And I'm the only one who loves you. You know that?" She didn't turn around.

I stayed silent for several minutes. Then I spoke.

"Yes, Betty. I know." My agreement shocked me.

Betty walked over to me and patted my hair.

"So very soft," she murmured.

She walked quietly into her room of dolls and closed the door. Suddenly I heard a moan, then a wail, then hysteria. I had never heard hysteria before. It came through the dawn like a quake, a sudden jolt that throws you to the floor. I heard screams, and the shelves holding her dolls being pulled off the wall. I heard each doll being pulled apart, thrown against the ceiling and its own clouds, stretched before her like religion, and summer, and the songs she wouldn't sing anymore, ever, not for God or me or a crowd. Then I heard her knees hit the floor, a wailing burping out like disease, and I knew she was rocking back and forth, holding onto nothing but herself. Then the sound of her crying muffled on a pillow. Then silence. By then the sun was out, and it was hot.

{ *sixteen* }

I WAS NOT invited to Frank's funeral, the memorial services, or his wake. These were held, free of charge to Betty, at his former place of employment, the Eternal Praise Funeral Home. Apparently this was one of the many privileges and perks employees at the Eternal were given.

It was August 17 by the time Betty had finished. I had no idea death took so much time, that it required preparations, parties, services, shopping for death clothes.

In those weeks I was kept at home, allowed to cook for myself, watch television, drink anything I wanted to out of the bar, which Betty now kept unlocked. She couldn't sleep. A margarita or a whiskey and beer now helped her get to sleep. Now she drank whiskey and beer, just like Frank. She would pour in the beer first, then gradually let the whiskey roll in the glass in gold, dreamy waves. Betty would watch this, scowl, then stir the glass into its right color, like old urine, then drink it down in one long stretch. I would turn away, because if I saw her face, it would have Frank's dead kisses on it, her eyes full of tears.

I drank when Betty was gone, which was all day and into the early evening. At first I took sips from a bottle of Heublein Manhattans, which had a color picture of a frosty drink with a woman with red lipstick above it, and she looked like she was having a great time. It was sweet as cough syrup, and it made me dizzy. I danced until I fell. Or until the dizziness made me think I was somewhere else, seeing things that didn't make sense.

I slept, then took more sips when I woke up, then giggled at the news, at Marge Condon in *Open House,* a television show where an old lady in a tight wig showed viewers how to make animals out of old cardboard toilet rolls, and how to sauté shrimp, then throw it into leftover macaroni and cheese for dinner. This was the only daytime woman's program on, besides soap operas, and I watched to find out the next step, what constituted a woman's mind and if it was right for me. Marge always had guests on; women who worked with the retarded and deaf, women who made sequined gowns, which were exotic, something only the Supremes, or movie stars, would wear. A woman named Trisha Fink held her sequined gown up to the studio lights for close to a minute, so we could ogle. Marge went "Ooh" and "Aah." She never changed the timbre of her voice, which was bored and low and whispery, the way she felt important women should speak.

For two weeks I lay on my back on Betty's couch, in the caustic breeze of her electric fan, and toasted Frank. I was drunk for two full weeks, and Betty didn't pay attention.

I tried to repair the dolls she had broken, and I fixed her shelves. Some dolls were easy. A little Elmer's Glue around their necks, but others had to be suspended on rolled-up towels and china until the glue took hold. I imagined myself Doctor Frankenstein, and now these dolls were repaired, staring at me with grateful faces, I would inject them with life. My favorite was a French doll that resembled a full-grown woman. Her porcelain arms were long and hollow, gloved with a silk fabric. Her hair was glued into a chignon that reeked of powder and nails. She looked like Georgia in her eighteenth-century French dress with tiny embroidered roses and actual bones underneath, keeping the skirt stiff and flounced. If she were real as my grandmother, she would hit someone with that dress as she walked by and they would certainly fall.

I still didn't like going into Betty's room of dolls. I would take them into the living room to fix them. That small shuttered room held an anger that I knew, could breathe in, and something else, a past. It was in the dolls sitting with clumsy china legs on thin board and never seeing daylight. They were never touched, never dusted. I thought in secret they spoke of me as one of them.

I began to have trouble remembering what my grandmother and my mother looked like. When I slept, alcohol rubbing my veins like a massage bed in a motel, my dreams didn't hold them. Once, I saw my mother walking away in a flowered dress. The only way I was certain it was her is that she was walking toward Bob.

I thought by the middle of August I would have heard from them. But there were no postcards, no Polaroids or notes written on perfumed ship stationery. I wanted to crease a tangible hello on my palms, rub it for good luck, and put it in my box under my bed on the porch.

But I dreamed of Betty. When I fell asleep before she came home, I dreamed Frank was in the closet, purple and quite dead, and that we had murdered him. He was banging on the door to get out and Betty held me, forcing me to open the door, saying we were murderers, that Frank had to be buried in the backyard. Brenda had become a mastiff with a foaming mouth. When I opened the door Brenda lunged at Betty, and I had to pull Frank out of the closet and drag him through the kitchen into the backyard. There was a hole full of water and I pushed him in. As he sank, water lilies began to form. Betty was screaming in the house, fighting off Brenda, and these water lilies were pink and white and smelled like jasmine. When a bee landed on one it grew teeth and swallowed the bee, then I laughed. I ran. I was terrified of a pond full of laughing water lilies. I ran until I could see the sun on the horizon, and I decided to look it into the eye, and keep running toward it, until I was bathed in white, until the spots under my eyes became my universe. Then I woke.

Betty was sitting in a black silk dress, with perspiration stains under her arms and around the collar.

"It's over." She was smoking, watching the white light come from the television.

"What time is it?" I asked. My head hurt from the bottle of Manhattans. The bottle was empty now, and I realized I would have to somehow break it when Betty was gone, then make a stain on the carpet with some water, and say I knocked it over by accident.

"It's midnight, L.P. You go back to sleep." She closed her eyes and took her black leather shoes off.

"Have you had anything to eat?"

"Yes," I lied.

"What did you have?" Her voice was distant.

"I made a sandwich." There wasn't any bread in the house. Only some cans of Hormel chili and Campbell's soup.

"That's good." Betty sounded like she was sleepwalking.

I liked this time of night. Air was mild and light. It was like a bath without water.

"I don't want to go back to sleep," I said softly, staring at Betty. I was tired of the couch. I wanted to go outside and look at the sky, and I told Betty that's what I wanted to do.

"All right," she said, surprised.

"Take my hand. We'll fix ourselves a drink and we'll sit outside. Frank liked that." Betty walked over to the liquor cabinet and began to pour herself a drink of whiskey and beer. Then she stood very still.

"I see you've polished off the Manhattans." Her back was turned to me and her voice sounded like it was going to break.

"Yes," I said, in my meekest, please-don't-be-angry, voice.

Betty began to laugh. It wasn't a full laugh, when something is funny, but a slow exhale, as if she realized what might be funny, and let it go as she breathed.

"Well," she countered. "You're still alive, aren't you?" I watched her walk into the kitchen and plop some ice into her drink, then ice in a glass for me. She handed it over firmly.

"Try the Piña Colada bottle, L.P. It's got coconut milk in it. It'll coat your stomach."

I opened the bottle of Heublein Piña Colada and poured it myself, not embarrassed at all, but proud. I took Betty's hand and we walked into the backyard.

"You fed Brenda, didn't you?" She looked puzzled.

"Sure," I said, and I had. Brenda was watching us from her dog house. She knew Frank was gone. She rolled over and went back to sleep. Brenda wasn't about to be bothered with Betty.

"Look up into the sky and say hello to Frank, honey. He's watching us," Betty said, jiggling the ice in her drink.

I did. It was a clear sky, littered with stars that didn't sparkle, or connect into dippers and lions. They looked like moonstones, and I thought I could look through them into the dull light that stabbed through the blackened wall above us. I could smell magnolias and night-blooming flowers that didn't have names. Night birds were scuttling over cacti and manzanita trees. Betty and I sat at the picnic bench and I felt like I could fly.

"You've been very grown up, keeping house for me

like this." Betty smiled at me. I heard crickets. She stared up at the sky again.

"It was a nice funeral, L.P.," she began, "and every-one you met was there. No children, though. It was a decision I had to make." She ran her hand over her neck.

"See, there are certain things only my kind should be at. You understand, honey?" I nodded my head. Betty's eyes twitched briefly, and she continued.

"I didn't want . . ." Her voice trailed, and she began again, taking a sip of Frank's drink. She let it sit in her mouth, then swallowed.

"I didn't think it was appropriate for you to see what death is. What a face looks like when the soul's walked. You're still a boy. You'll see enough later." Her voice seemed almost serene. I heard two cats fighting and growling in the next yard.

Betty's eyes turned away from the sky, and focused on the grass. I had watered it one day completely naked, and it had been fun.

"It's a lot of work. It's all work. It never stops," Betty said, bending down and running her hand over the al-most dead grass.

Betty had a spray of gardenias attached to the lapel of her black suit and she suddenly became aware of them, taking the spray and attaching it to her hair.

"If you touch them, they yellow. But if you don't touch them, and hold them by the leaf, they stay white. It's the prettiest white I know." She moved her head around and I could see the gardenias in the night air, held by a trance, whiter than the stars, glistening like ripe pearls on Betty's head. She knew how to wear gardenias. And she was wearing them for me.

"You should have seen the flowers, L.P. Carmelita made sure they were fresh. All of them from fields a mile away. You would have thought the heat would have killed them. I always forget how crafty the Japanese are. They have greenhouses air-conditioned in the summer and heated in the winter. Those are the flowers that grow perfect. They don't have any worries. No dust, no fire. Always a rainy mist that sprays on them on every hour. It must be nice to grow and live when you have everything you need," Betty said, sighing.

I nodded my head in agreement. I wondered what I needed to grow up perfect, and as I sipped my Piña Colada, I realized I had it here. The night drew itself as a Van Gogh, deliberate swirls and pockets of nothingness around us. I was certain if I looked through the dark I would see flowers that were crooked and stung and, like my dreams, they would talk. Catch flies and laugh.

I let Betty talk. She was on the outside looking in, and this was familiar to me. She had to count everything, as I did, make lists, note times and burials, who attended, who should be sent thank you notes, what kind of notes to send.

"The same band played for Frank that plays at the Blue Note on Saturday night. Skeleton was there. So were Marty and Ernesto, guys I knew on the road close to twenty-five years ago. Frank never liked any of them. But it was fitting. It was."

She put her feet up on the redwood bench and wiggled her toes.

"I drank a lot of champagne. We all drank champagne. And there was sandwiches with Jewish meats. They're the best you know. I had my own Cadillac limousine. A white one that they say was used for Barry Goldwater. Bulletproof glass, a bar in the back, the works."

I was beginning to feel slightly drunk and liked it. I was happy that Betty was happy, and calm. No longer crying, as she had for many days. Her eyes were no longer pink and puffed, and in the haze of the desert moon their color was sharp, alive, distinct with a future.

"I got life insurance, L.P. Frank left me money with life insurance. It means we'll be able to live all right, without any worries about money." She smiled at me. I didn't understand.

"Am I living with you now, Betty?" I asked. The skin on my arms began to tingle. One of my feet had fallen asleep. When Betty heard this question, she stood up and stretched like a cat.

"Would you like to, honey? Would you like to live with Betty? I'd take real good care of you and love you till I die. No one loves you like I do, L.P. See, I know what you are, and I don't care. We all got to live with something. You'll grow up to be good and kind. It's written on your hands. On your face and the way you do things for others." She bent over and gave me a hug. She smelled like Lily of the Valley and polished wood. I broke away and ran inside, burying my head on my bed on the back porch. I began to cry, then throw up. I didn't comprehend why I was crying, but I knew I was drunk.

Betty came in and saw I had thrown up on the floor, and brought a wet towel from the kitchen and, on her knees, wiped it up.

"I shouldn't have let you drink. But you might as well know what it is. Now, no more sneaking in the liquor cabinet." She touched my forehead and I refused to look at her.

Where was Violet? Why didn't she love me anymore? I wasn't black. I didn't want to be black. I wanted to be rich and famous and look like women who descend in planes in big sunglasses. Women who always were in a hurry to get someplace expensive and secret, where they could plot marriages to kings, plot parties where the most beautiful people in the world came, and admired them, and everyone knew each other by name. I didn't want to live in South Phoenix anymore, and I didn't want to know about dead people, because I was one of them, or about friends I wouldn't bother to see again, because we had seen the forbidden, and that would send us to hell.

I could feel Betty's hand on my forehead and I was spinning into a black well. My heart was beating fast and I was surprised, somewhere in my livid spirals, that my heart was beating at all. It had been taken away and not given back. I didn't know how to find it, and right now, there was no sky to fly into to look. The nights birds began to sing. Betty pulled a thin cotton blanket over me, murmuring, "Sleep it off, child, and forget." Inside my mind a sun was rising, extinguishing this night and the fact that Betty knew me for what I was, and I tried to look into it, but it had no warmth or light.

seventeen

THE NEXT DAY Betty fixed me breakfast.

"We've got to get on with our lives," she said cheerfully. Everything she said had "we" in it, and I was still doubtful about whether I was Betty's now, to do with as she pleased. Breakfast was good. I peeled two bananas and ate them, along with eggs and toast.

"When does my mama come home?" I asked stridently. Nothing was making sense to me.

Betty became silent and washed dishes. She wiped her hands and put some Ponds Cream on them, then spoke.

"We've got shopping to do, L.P. We're finally going to have a garden in the back." I was stunned that she wouldn't answer my question.

"When is my mama coming home?" I repeated. My voice was loud and I could hear how high it was.

"Don't be obnoxious. Get dressed. We're going shopping."

Betty ran her hands over her marcelled hair, letting their dampness keep it in place. She sighed, not looking at me, and spoke.

"Miss Violet will be back on September first."

"How did you know?" I demanded. I was furious no one had told me dates. "When does my grandmother come home?"

"The day before. And you go home on the second. But you told me you didn't want to go home. You said you wanted to stay here with me." Betty's voice was slow, almost pleading.

"I did not! I did not!" I was screaming. Then I saw her cry. I became quiet and walked over to her. I put my hand in hers.

"I want to go home now, Betty. Can't I wait there? It's only a week."

"No. You're under my charge. I thought you liked it here."

"I do."

"Well?" Suddenly Betty's eyes were cold.

I was stuck. I said nothing, only shrugged, and went to change into some shopping clothes. She looked at me the same way I had seen black people look at white people when they had to step out of white people's way in front of expensive restaurants and in front of movie theaters.

It occurred to me that Betty didn't like me all along. But I dismissed that. She wanted me to stay with her forever. She wanted to be my mother. I shuddered, thinking perhaps all of this had been planned by my family to get rid of me. That they were letting me down slowly.

If that was true, then I would live with Betty. But I wanted to know more. I called out from the back porch.

"Betty, where did Mama go on her honeymoon?"

I could see Betty sitting at the kitchen table, smoking a Kool and leaning her face in the direction of the fan in the living room. It was going to be extremely hot. I had taken my salt tablets at breakfast. I saw Betty close her eyes in the faint breeze.

"Your mama told Miss Georgia she was going to San Francisco, then Canada. But your mama and Bob went down to Rocky Point in Mexico. They rented a house."

"Why did she have to lie?" I asked.

"She always lies." Betty stubbed her cigarette out.

I froze. The idea that my mother lied was completely foreign to me. She had always taught me to tell the truth no matter what. That even white lies grow and destroy. I suddenly felt stupid and full of hate.

Of course, it was entirely possible Betty was lying as well. But the geography of her remark made me realize she wasn't. She was a Negro widow sitting in Phoenix, taking care of a white boy and it was the end of August. She was a Negro widow sitting in her kitchen, near a reliable fan, and she could still smell her husband in every room. There was no reason to tell lies. Or talk at all.

In that transparent web of menthol cigarette smoke and finalities, Betty's voice became horrible and distant. She sounded like she was handing me small poisons, that

I could store away one at a time, until my skin was devoid of any color. Until my resistance was high. I

could be half dead, but I could take any poison, just dose me with it, and I'd live.

I was silent as I put on my shorts and Hawaiian shirt and thongs. I could hear the fan going back and forth, the sound of Betty's nails tapping the table.

"Does Mama lie to me?" I asked in a quiet voice. I wondered if Betty could hear me.

"All the time," she said, equally quiet.

"What about Nana?" I continued.

"Miss Georgia don't lie, L.P. But she's mean. You know that. You're too smart to begin with. Why ask me these questions?" Her voice was rising. I looked out the screen and saw Brenda crying for Frank.

"Because I want to know."

Betty chuckled. My forehead was sweating.

"That's fair." She got up, and came to the back porch. "Brenda's going today."

I knew Betty was getting rid of Brenda, that she had promised her to a family down the street after Frank died. But I thought she would let Brenda stay until I left. I had begun to like Brenda. I let her lick my bare feet when I played in the yard. I shrieked when Brenda dribbled saliva all over them.

"Damn nuisance dog," Betty muttered.

Once in the car, our first stop was to give Brenda away. Brenda was sitting in the backseat, being quite calm, as though she knew. When Betty let Brenda out, she immediately rolled on her new front lawn and peed.

The family came out and played with her, giving Betty a small roll of one dollar bills, which Betty turned down with a wave of her hand. I expected Brenda to cry and look back at us, but she didn't. We ceased to exist. Dogs were just like people. Something better comes along and they run with a wet nose and their tongue hanging.

The sky was white hot, and we quickly got back in the car. Betty looked me up and down, then started the car and pulled away.

"See how easy it is to get rid of something you don't like?" Betty said.

I knew she was talking about me. But I didn't say anything. She had already been cross with me that morning. Betty began to laugh so hard her voice squeaked and tears formed.

"Jesus Christ, that dog was a pain in the ass!" She laughed so hard she had to stop the car, and I began to laugh, too. She motioned for a Kleenex and I tried to give her one. I was laughing so hard I dropped the box on the floor of the car, which made her laugh even harder.

"I want three orange trees. And a lemon. And a grapefruit," Betty said. We were at a Japanese nursery near the flower fields. Betty was very animated, gesturing with her hands.

"I want them big, with fruit. And I'll pay to have one of your boys plant them, today if you can. I got cash."

The Japanese man, dressed in overalls with no shirt, smiled and nodded his head. He took Betty out in the glare to limitless rows of orange trees and pots. Betty

told me to go look at the flower fields. To be back in
fifteen minutes. I had dreamed of doing this. I ran, as
fast as possible in the heat, down the road half a mile
and came upon them. I held my breath.

It was like staring into the sun to see spots. Electric
yellow fields of stock rolled like wheat in the desert sun.
Splashes of lavender and pink crested the borders and,
to my eyes, the fields were at least a mile long. The first
thing I wanted to do was count exactly how many
flowers went in each line. I began to sneeze from the
pollen and I didn't care. I jumped over a low barbed
wire fence I reasoned was there to keep animals out,
not people, and I began to lose myself quickly.

This was the astonishment I had waited for all summer. I lived to be astonished, and I hadn't found it in
the eucalyptus groves, on the Fourth of July, in Davis'
basement, or drinking Heublein Manhattans. I could see
Japanese women in wide straw hats bending over, pick-
ing stock with bushels tied to their backs. It was as if
flowers grew out of them, and they were moving plants.
I rolled in a gully of crushed and trampled flowers, letting their scent soak into me, seeing how the pollen
stained my tanned skin. I stared up at the sky. It moved
in circles. I prayed to not one but several Gods that I
had created, women without faces who controlled kindness and magic, and I told them to let me stay here and
never go back.

Then I heard Betty's car honk. I stood up and saw
her walk up to the fence, looking for me. I ran toward
her. I wanted to bring her in this place and let her see

for herself the colors. I was Dorothy in *The Wizard of Oz* and I knew if I didn't leave soon, I would fall asleep.

When she saw me she stood rigid and her eyes got large. Her mouth opened and I saw her teeth from quite a distance.

I didn't realize, as I ran toward her, that I was covered with pollen and sap. I was pink and lavender and bright yellow. My hair was covered with leaves and dust and my clothes were smeared with manure.

"It's so pretty!" I squealed, standing in front of her.

She began to laugh the same way I had heard in the car.

"You smell like a French whore." Betty pinched her nose with her fingers, still laughing. Then she began to hiccup. I was sweating through the pollen and sap. My Hawaiian shirt was stuck to my back. Like I was swimming in my shirt, and got out of the pool, and didn't dry off. Then I knew I had been swimming, without water, using only air and earth and honey.

We got into her car and she rolled down the back windows, waving her hand around.

"Jesus, you stink!" Betty had become hysterical. I knew it because her laughter sounded like a machine gun and she couldn't stop. Her voice got higher and higher until she sounded like helium escaping a tank.

"L.P.'s turned into a rainbow. My little boy is a rainbow!"

She kept laughing until the hiccups were gone. Betty fanned herself, tapped her chest, held her breath, lit cigarettes, laughed. I touched my hands to my face, my nose. I felt deliriously happy. I imagined I was wearing a crown of flowers; daisies and passion flowers and mums. Each flower sang the night bird cantata, Betty's laughter in the afternoon glare was a wind, and I was loved, unconditionally, by the sun, the irrigated soil, by the largesse of everything around me that claimed to have a soul.

At dusk the Japanese came and planted her trees. Betty stood like an army general, directing them to exact spots, crossing her arms and pointing constantly.

I stood next to her. This was exciting.

"Frank never liked citrus. But I did. I saved for these trees for a long time. Now they're mine." Betty said this to me with assurance. She put her arm around my shoulder.

"Now we'll always have fruit to eat." She looked into my eyes and became very serious.

"L.P., I'm not stupid. You'll be in your home soon. But you remember. Remember these trees. When you're bigger than me you'll know where the sweetest oranges in Phoenix are. And lemons for your iced tea. And grapefruit for your breakfast. You remember."

I smiled. This was one kindness that made sense, that didn't have another face. I was surprised at how large her trees were. When the Japanese had finished, they looked like they had been there for many years.

By night the backyard was dramatic and scented with lemon blossoms, the husk spray of citrus and the oniony smell of its thick, waxy leaves. We sat at the picnic table and ate barbecued chicken.

Betty tore down Brenda's dog house and threw the loose boards next to her garbage on the front drive.

"Praise God that's finished," she said, turning the hose on her hands.

We played Scrabble outside, and Betty lit one of Frank's tiki torches so we could see.

"Those'll be the next to go. From here on, I'll use candlelight. I'll build a patio and have wrought iron chairs." Betty spoke wistfully and only half to me.

By midnight I had fallen asleep, my head on the picnic table. I heard music. When I looked up, I saw Betty had brought out the hi-fi with an extension cord and was playing one of her songs. She was dancing by herself, through her new, perfumed orchard, turning herself around, her arms swinging in an arc in front of her. She was dancing with Frank, with the night air, with ghosts and bees and citrus blossoms.

Betty drifted through her trees, sometimes bending down, then extending her arms up toward the clouded moon. It looked like a fox trot, a slow dance where she moved the way she wanted to, serene, with a record that automatically played itself over. She was singing and she was young. She was a ballerina.

I followed, wanting to show her how I thought a ballerina would dance. I danced on point, right behind her, brushing my hair against the oranges and leaves of low-hanging branches. I spun myself until I fell down, then counted moving stars.

"You know what, L.P.?" Betty's voice moved with her through the trees.

"What?" I drawled.

"I'm sixty-one years old and I'm dancing."

The breeze shook the oranges. One fell on the ground. I saw Betty's feet continually shuffle back and forth to the music. I saw the Big Dipper and it sparkled like rhinestones. I saw two spiders fight in the dark. I realized that only goddesses controlled such magic, and that they could be reached. When God was too busy to listen to me, they would cluster in my background and wait.

eighteen

IT WAS THE last day of August. In two days I would be back with my family. They had never corresponded, or called. I assumed they were happy, possibly in love, shopping and eating exotic foods. But they weren't doing it with me.

I helped Betty plant new roses in her garden. And strange vegetables I had never heard of, like jicama and cilantro and chives, which she explained were nothing more than onions.

We didn't discuss Violet and Georgia. We didn't discuss Frank. They became an invisible pocket of air where words disappeared, trailed off when started, and not formed again. There was no reason to speak ill of the dead. Betty knew my childhood had ended. She spoke to me like an adult, and I was happy. She listened to me.

"Betty, why do people marry?" I asked, my knees in the soil next to her. It was a little after dawn and I was wide awake. We could plant these limpid hours, before the sun grew claws. The flowers seemed grateful. Their leaves were firm and their blossoms didn't wilt at dawn. It was an anesthesia, the mint-scented gas you breathe before black, and the rest of the day was still.

"Because they love each other. You know that. Hand me the mums." Betty's hunch didn't look like one when she bent over, digging in the crystal desert dirt with her trowel. She found a piece of quartz and gave it to me.

"But what if they don't love each other?" I asked.

"Then they don't get married."

"What about money?" I questioned her innocently. I knew better than to say anything about Georgia, but I was curious. Did Georgia marry for money, and if so, why? What came out of it? My mother didn't. She had said she married for love, to give me a father figure, but he wasn't much of anything. Digging with Betty in an August dawn, I tried to remember what he looked like, and I couldn't. Betty knew I was talking about my grandfather. She thought for a moment, then arched her eyebrows.

"People that marry for money are in love with money. So, somehow they are in love, and they never change. So there is a reason."

I listened to her and pursed my lips. It made sense, but I expected more drama to her answer.

"Why did you get married?"

I knew I had said the wrong thing. I wasn't supposed to mention Frank, but I promised myself not to, to keep

Betty from thinking. Once she lapsed and thought a lot about Frank, and sat at her kitchen table for a full day. She never ate, drank anything. Just smoked Kools. It had become so still in her kitchen, when I came in from the living room, I had to wave smoke away just to see her.

Betty put her trowel carefully down and rubbed her arms. I saw she was trying to form the right words, without proper names or the treachery of convenient memory. She wanted to tell me the truth.

"Hand me that iced tea." Betty took a few sips, then began to speak in a simple, low voice.

"I was married four times, L.P. The first three men were bastards. They spent my money and I let them. The fourth—" Betty paused. "I married because I thought I was pregnant and the doctor told me I was four months gone. Could you believe it? I didn't even know. I got married. I lost the child in a motel room in El Paso when I was playing a club whose name I don't . . . it was the Jade Palace. A Chinese restaurant for coloreds with a jazz club in the back. Jesus, what a trap."

I was fascinated, and motioned for her to continue.

"Sometimes you hemorrhage when you lose a little one. I couldn't stop. I had to cancel my club dates. Suddenly I didn't have any work. I had to get married and stay put. It was okay. Sometimes you discover, L.P., that one part of your life ends, another begins, and you keep your mouth shut."

The sun's rays had turned into the beginnings of morning, a throbbing yellow that erased shadows. Crickets stopped chirping. We could hear cars on the freeway across the Gila River.

Betty stood up.

"That's all I can do today." She said this sadly, and I stood up too. We would spend the rest of the day inside. The weather man said on the late news temperatures could reach one hundred twenty degrees.

Following her in, I thought about my ends and beginnings. I knew they were related. They were mother and son, mother and daughter, fathers who stayed away. Beginnings end, and endings start something fresh, a light that is tangible, a spirit I could hold to my chest, then let go. Death and ghosts who could be conjured by speaking their names, a simple reference to anything hurtful and hushed; these were ends, roads out littered with nails and whitewashed signs. Beginnings were never as obvious.

My ends were listed with sunsets. My mother turning around in a telephone booth, crying in the middle of a shabby desert. The sunset in back of us when we drove home covered our hair in hot vermilion light. Coming home from Davis' house, cumulus clouds attained peach and silver rims, then darkening purples as Samuel and Grover turned their backs and walked inside their nests, their mothers outlined with a sharpened charcoal pencil. Or Indian women who methodically packed their sidewalk suitcases of silver belts and chunky rings when the sun turned yellow as a macaw. Then the continual dusk when Betty and I spoke, its softened smoke lilting through baby orchards and the lingering odor of an unwanted dog.

Beginnings came with sound. And women. The rustle of cocktail dresses and click of high heels, the way they opened doors and air jumped, the sound of black beads being passed through their fingers, rings played with, voices lowering to hush when men were spoken of, uncommon laughter that precedes tears and the hysteria of daily psalms.

Wind erased days with the brush of palm fronds. When the early evening winds came, women would speak louder, perfume would become noticeable and floating. Women decided fates, their nails tapping windowpanes and tables in a Morse code, their children in shuttered rooms, waiting for these sounds to become kind and resplendent.

I knew when I was born I came in a sack and a string. The string turned into a stick and the sack became luggage with locks, stored in closets and seldom used. The stick became my grandfather's walking cane. The stick became a rod holding silk curtains in Georgia's bedroom, the elongated feather duster Betty used to clean her chandelier. The stick became the spike under my mother's favorite pair of Italian high-heeled shoes, the spike that broke off and was repaired, then broke off again and was put away in tissue paper, in a box she would perhaps open twenty, thirty years later, saying to herself, "God, those were gorgeous shoes."

That night I drew a map of where I began and where I ended. I promised myself not to manufacture. No Sophia Loren, even though I loved to draw her oval, heavily made up eyes. I used a large piece of tissue paper from Betty's tissue paper drawer, and I taped it to the kitchen table. Betty came in from time to time to watch me draw.

"What in hell is that, L.P.?"

"It's a map," I said guardedly.

"Of Phoenix?" she asked, peering over my shoulder.

"Kind of," I said. "It's everything up to now." I tried to sound mysterious.

I started with my pink apartment building and wrote BEGIN HERE. I found some pink glitter and rubbed glue, then dusted the apartment building with glitter. I drew roads like Central Avenue and McDowell Road, the hotel restaurant my father took me to when I was five. I drew Indian women and put angel wings on their shoulders, and positioned them floating at all four corners of the page. I drew brown men with pickaxes and white shirts and shovels on highways leading out of Phoenix like spiderwebs. I wrote where the ends came.

I drew the Gila River cutting through Phoenix like a frantic reptile. Then I drew South Phoenix. I sketched with crayon gold pagodas and squares of flower fields, Davis' Spanish house with willows and wind. I drew the Desert Bowl and put a bowling ball on the roof that was supposed to spin around.

I drew the eucalyptus grove near the river. I had almost no space left. In a tiny space in the lower left-hand corner I drew Betty's house, with orange trees and roses. Above her house I wrote END HERE. Then, all over the page, I sprinkled another jar of glitter to make it look like the Fourth of July.

When I finished I realized I had forgotten to draw myself. I looked over the sheet of tissue paper, trying to find one space where I could sketch my face. The willow trees and highways and Indian women took up too much room. There was no space for me. Tomorrow would be September 1.

Summer was over.

I IMAGINED VIOLET a deep brown, wearing flowers in her hair when she got back. Perhaps a Mexican silver cross studded with amethysts and alexandrites, the kind hanging in Tijuana stores, would adorn her neck. She would be young and giddy and smile. Her lips would be glossy pink, her eyes made up like Delores del Rio. She would tell me she loved me, that she was my mother and she missed me. The apartment would be filled with bright paper flowers and there would be a piñata in my bedroom, filled with Mexican chocolate and strawberries rolled in rock sugar. We would speak in perfect Spanish, even down to the Barcelona lisp, then revert to English. It would be our secret, and we would speak rapidly until Georgia came in the room, and she would be furious she didn't understand what we were saying.

I imagined Bob with a sunburn, dressed in wicked yellow and purple stripes, never taking his sunglasses off. He would shake my hand, smile, and tell me he brought me a present. A large stuffed alligator, almost three feet long, that I could put on my desk as a trophy. And a wallet with my initials burnt on stiff, beaten leather. I decided I would be nice to him, and that we would be friends.

Together they would tell me they made friends in Mexico, that soon we would visit, and perhaps even live there for a while. My mother would show me pictures of the Sea of Cortez, and confide in me how she saw whales and dolphins in the evening sun, but all she could think of was how much she wanted me there.

Then upstairs, with my grandmother, I would receive gifts from Denmark, maybe even Paris, rings and watches and boxes with keys. Georgia and Henry Adams would admire my sketches, approve of my summer with Betty, and give her a raise and a pretty cocktail dress, one with a satin wrap to cover her hump. Betty would laugh, try it on, and come out looking very glamorous, her neck arched like an opera singer, her head ready for a tiara.

I imagined going back to school, and telling the friends I didn't have that shortly I would be moving to a big plantation in the Yucatán, where it was solid jungle, with its own beach, and I could pick coconuts and bananas whenever I wanted. I would write to them, of course. But I planned never to write, not even a one-peso postcard. And everyone would tell stories about me that got bigger as they grew older. In high school, I would be the one everyone was waiting for to come back. Girls would acknowledge I was handsome and rich. Boys would talk about how I was muscular and had a beard. Stepping out of the lazy surf, my body covered with foam, I would talk to the sun, tell it to be kind to the children in Phoenix, for they were not as happy or fortunate as I.

Betty dropped me off on the third floor. When we unlocked the apartment I felt a stillness that could mean something hollow and wrong had descended into my air. Mother was back, but not here.

"She's upstairs with Miss Georgia. You come up shortly, after you unpack." Betty turned to leave, and I touched her arm. She was wearing her white maid's uniform, and she seemed uncomfortable.

"Is Bob here?" I asked.

Betty knitted her eyebrows together.

"I'll be upstairs, L.P. You go on and unpack."

Betty quickly left. I had one suitcase and a box, which I took into my room. I could smell myself here, again, with the shades up and the sun smearing its corners with heat. Opening my suitcase, I realized I never bought anything for my family, no souvenirs. I was always taught to buy something as a gift when you travel. As a memory. I remembered everything I had counted, written down, and sketched. But I stood very still. I had left my map taped to Betty's kitchen table.

The same silence I had felt when Frank died and Betty disappeared into funerals, and the mist of sympathy, made itself known to me here. All I heard was air-conditioning turn on and off, the same signals that stayed with me in August. Warning signals for swift currents, drowning pools, undertows.

I should have brought home a plastic water lily from the Baptist Church pond, or a dried willow branch from Davis' house, or a river rock from the Gila River. I had the piece of quartz Betty gave me when she was digging her garden. That was all.

My grandmother and mother made a big deal about how lucky I was, how very few children had the comforts of life that I had. I was taught that everything I was given, even the smallest present, I should appreciate, say, "Thank you," over and over. I stopped saying, "Thank you," when I noticed my mother threw away most of my gifts, and my grandmother packed everything I gave in a closet in the seventh-floor apartment. Not unlike a time capsule in a tomb.

I went to my window and, with a chill on my arms, counted the date palms in the next-door dirt lot. It was time to get back to living, as Betty had said. They were all there. My mother and I would be allowed to stay. And Bob, too, if he was nice and did what Georgia wanted.

I remembered what I felt staring at my dark room six weeks ago, when I was outside and pressing my face into its shadows, and I felt like I was choking. I still felt it. That whatever was here, didn't live here anymore.

When I opened my desk drawer, all my papers and pencils were gone. I opened another drawer and my watercolor paint set and magazine photos of Sophia Loren and Marilyn Monroe were gone, too. I opened my closet doors and saw three suits I had never seen before. The rest of my clothes were gone. There were suitcases on the floor beneath them. Three new suitcases, each smaller than the other, with my initials on them.

I began to cry. I was not in control, and my hands were shaking. I wiped my eyes and decided to be strong. I knew then all the fears were here, they were walking beside me.

Running into the living room, I checked to see if there were any signs of Mexico. A bright blanket or a paper flower. The apartment was the same, but it felt like a hotel. Maybe we moved upstairs with Georgia, or into the seventh-floor apartment. I thought this was now a guest apartment for guests we didn't have. Maybe the Phoenix Towers was becoming a hotel, and tomorrow the doors to 3-B would open and travelers would come, staying overnight, never longer, invisible fragrances that I would grow to understand.

I shook my head, then walked into my mother's bedroom. It was still aqua, but the pictures of Bob had been taken down. One picture frame holding a photo of me had been replaced with a color 8 x 10 of my mother in a white fox and pearls. She was smiling at the camera, directly into it, and her eye shadow was blue.

All the rest of my photographs were still facedown, in a stack on the bottom shelf. I picked them up, looked through them, then put them in a circle around the photograph of my mother. Then I left the room, went into my bathroom, washed my face and hands, and went upstairs.

I realized my life came in shorthand. A series of dots and dashes, crossed-out letters and running ink. I could create words from these hieroglyphics, but it was hard work. I could write sincerely and with best wishes at the bottom of the page, but the rest was mysterious, a catatonia. It was easier to count and draw, memorize by lip, or close my eyes and feel my way through it, until I was sure of everything around me.

These methods vanished when I knocked on Georgia's door. I heard Betty shout out, "Come in." I opened the door to the kitchen. We never used the front door. It was down a private hall with a chandelier, a painting of my grandmother in a blue fox over a French sidetable, and two candelabras with tapered ivory candles that were never lit. That was the door Georgia opened when she was dressed in tight silk and gloves, when her face was made up and the jewelry was on. That was the Country Club door.

"I'm thirsty," I said. I wanted to say something that sounded normal, like it was still late May.

Betty said nothing. She was upset, and I didn't know why. She glared at me, something she never did, went to the refrigerator and poured me a ginger ale. She dropped two ice cubes in it and handed it to me.

"Can I have some more ice? It's really hot." I huffed to make sure she could see I was hot. She rolled her eyes, and plopped three more ice cubes in my glass.

"Are you mad at me?" I inquired softly, sipping my ginger ale. I had learned to ask this question, then immediately apologize for anything. It made things smooth. I realized I hadn't done this all summer. Things were back to normal.

Betty softened, shaking her head.

"You better go inside, L.P."

"I don't want to. Something's wrong," I whispered.

Betty nodded her head.

"Something is wrong, L.P. Listen, I'll be right here, behind you. You remember all the fun we had? Just think about it." Her voice drifted and she went back to the sink when she heard Georgia's voice.

I stared at Betty. I hadn't seen her for maybe a half an hour. In the sleek pink light of Georgia's kitchen, wearing a white dress with an apron, she looked drained, her eyes muddy, incapable of her powers to absorb the colors around her. I marveled at how Betty's could change color from yellow-green to yellow, then even emerald. In the shade of her living room, they became feline, darting ovals that glittered. Now I saw rings under her eyes. She wasn't allowed to make up when she worked. I discovered what her shadowed rooms were for. I thought about how she danced around her orange trees. Her legs seemed stiff in front of me now, append-ages destined for complaint. She wiped her hands on a dish towel and faced the wall, not looking at me.

"I said go on in." Her voice was decisive and smooth.

"They don't want me anymore, do they? I'm going to live with you?" I asked, still whispering.

Betty jerked her thumb toward the shuttered swing door leading to the dining and living room. Her jaw was clenched. She kept folding and refolding her dish towel.

My grandmother's voice drifted in like poisoned smoke. I felt the essence of failure in my stomach. I knew I had failed just by being, and I was to become a buried thing, without initiation or permanence. I made myself far away as I reached to swing the door open. Something tainted and prophetic glided over me like gauze. I felt the stillness ready to amputate, telling me I must remember swinging this door open, finding something fierce and without truth. I wasn't in Phoenix, but another country, rummaging in a different skin. In another country I would finally send postcards, buy souvenirs, and this place was forgotten.

As the door swung open, I expected a white neon cross, a movie theater chandelier glowing, a lurid calendar of deserts and childhood places to be marked down with the blood of a purposely pricked finger, thick as paint. I expected to smell the Atlantic and Pacific Oceans, glamorous voices speaking in tongues and romances foreign, abstract, evil. My hair was blowing in a rooftop wind and my eyes were closed. I was ready to jump, twitching over a sea of late summer air. I was already packed, passport in hand, traveling in a captured silence, absorbing every indistinct color and thing that has flown. And I thought, I am never coming back.

My mother was wearing orange slacks and white silk cowgirl blouse. Her hair was messy and she had on a Pucci scarf that she had wrapped up like a turban. She didn't smell of Mexico. And she didn't have any movie star makeup on.

I studied my grandmother. Georgia didn't look rested. She fidgeted on her Spanish velvet sofa that had come from her house in Washington, D.C., the one Truman had sat on, and Perle Mesta, and countless ambassadors from tiny countries with no influence. She had on a housecoat of leopard and tropical flowers done in pleats.

She had her makeup on, and a turban, flat shoes with bows. She kept clearing her voice and sipping Diet Rite Cola.

They hadn't seen me silently glide into the room, standing at the far side, behind the dining room table. My mother kept her face to the picture window. She walked back and forth, shaking her head, then stopped, not looking at my grandmother, her face a few inches from the glass, then started walking again. Georgia cleared her throat again, took a sip of her drink, began to speak, then stopped. Another sip, glaring at my mother. Then her hand to her throat, then another sip. Silence.

The room was startling blue. I had forgotten it in full light. I expected boxes and gifts scattered on the furniture, furs thrown on club chairs. But it was the same as when Betty and I had visited it during the summer. In the entrenched sky beyond my mother's silhouette, a funnel cloud had formed in the east, then quickly dissipated. I promised myself not to speak until they saw me. It saddened me. I wanted to burst into the room with hugs, laughter.

I knew then, I had yet to move into this house.

Georgia spoke first.

"I leave for New York tomorrow. You have to tell him."

My mother sighed.

"I need him." Violet spoke about me. I was puzzled. They always referred to me as L.P. Suddenly I was him.

"I hate flying, Violet. You know that. You know what I'm going through." My grandmother took a sip of her Diet Rite and continued. "Right now you're a mess. You failed again. But then, I'm not surprised."

Violet began to sob, her face turned to the window.

"I told you time and time again he was a mistake. He was a weak man. Stay away from them. You want men you feel sorry for. Don't ever bother trying to help a sorry man. You lose," Georgia said, quite confidently.

"I'm so tired." Violet said this as a whisper, at a different pitch than I had ever heard. She sounded like a little girl who just got over the flu.

My grandmother groaned.

"For Christ sake, pull yourself up and be a lady. I am so damn bored of bailing you out. I'm tired, too, honey." Georgia lowered her head and twirled the gold rope around her neck. Her voice became guttural.

"My grandson is going places."

My mother began to throw her hands up in a gesture of disgust, but they stayed only halfway up, suspended like hummingbirds, twitching in anger. Slowly they turned into fists, then dropped to her side.

"God give me strength," Violet muttered.

"What was that, little girl?" My grandmother jumped on Violet's whispered oath. Georgia knew how not to let things pass. I saw the back of her head move slightly, then pull back. Wisps of hair not bound in her turban slid down her neck. She shifted her weight over on the sofa and continued to speak.

"As long as you're in my house . . ."

"Sometimes I think I'll die here," my mother interrupted, almost a hiss.

My grandmother was ready.

"So leave, Violet. Go. Have fun."

My mother began to sob again. I couldn't understand cruelty. I knew it was an abstract, a careless thing. Children were cruel and they were able to forget the next day. When adults were cruel, they planned it in advance. They grew their cruelties like Betty grew roses, beautifully wrapped reminders that had to be watered, cultivated, then cut.

I understood women like cruelty. It was their tissue paper, their new summer dress, a reason. It was the when and how to prepare each new cruelty, blue as a tattoo, a pinch that leaves bruises on skin. Each new sorrow became a list. An elixir. They would drink from it. Base their escapes, loves, damages on it.

My grandmother didn't stop. She liked being on a roll.

"You don't even know what time of day it is, sugar."

I heard Betty shuffling uncomfortably behind the kitchen door. She was listening, too. I knew she saw me through the slats. I knew she was saying on dry lips, "Not yet, L.P., see for yourself, not yet."

My mother began to shriek, staring out at Phoenix, refusing to turn to her mother. It was a subdued, calculated shriek, her voice jabbing the air with a diminished staccato. Violet knew how to have a fight behind closed doors. She knew how not to let anyone hear. Georgia had taught her.

"You can't do this to him. You know he's different."

"What do you mean 'different'?"

"You know." My mother was shaking.

"No, I don't know, Violet, why don't you tell me?"

my grandmother said curiously. It was the curiosity of people in cars passing by an accident on the freeway.

"Mother, for God's sake." Violet leaned on one hip and wiped away her wet cheeks.

"I know this. I pay for his education. I buy his clothes, feed you and him. You can't even cook. I'm more of a mother to him than you could ever be." My grandmother said this as though she were holding something back. Something in her clenched palms that she would pass back and forth, like a magician, ordering my mother to guess which hand. And Violet would always lose.

Violet interrupted Georgia, her chest heaving. She jabbed her finger in the cool air, pointing repeatedly at Georgia.

"L.P.'s a pansy. If you can't see it, you're blind. Jesus, Mother, I've dated fags. You thought they were going to marry me."

"That's not true." My grandmother's head began to lightly shake. "He's very well bred, that's all."

"Why do you think I married Bob? For the laughs? I've read queers get that way because of women. L.P. needed a man. You know what Bob said to me when he left? Do you?" Violet's voice rose.

"No." Georgia's voice was quiet, intent.

"Two weeks into our marriage. We're having a great time. Then all of a sudden the subject of my only child comes up. Bob says he doesn't think he can raise someone like L.P. He says this with a smile on his face. He says 'Why don't you put him in one of those special places where they burn ideas out of children's heads?' He says he wants his own son, a real boy. I say I don't want any more children, one was enough. Bob says, 'What about when L.P. hits puberty? What then?' He says he doesn't want to wake up with L.P.'s mouth on his cock."

My mother's voice had become ugly. She continued crying. Georgia said nothing. My face had become white. Suddenly everything I had imagined this summer was gone. Magic was meaningless. I wasn't dancing with Betty. I wasn't in China. I was an evil horrible entity. An aberration that people spoke of with a shudder. I saw myself as that woman in the hospital when Frank died, turning and saying, "You peeked."

My mother continued.

"We kept going. I should say, I kept going. We went to Mexico. I had to pay for everything." Violet's hands touched the glass of the picture window, then balled into fists again. "It was no tropical paradise, that I can tell you. I couldn't drink the water. We stayed drunk on margaritas. All I remembered were flies and wet sheets. And rain clouds in the morning. Sun in the afternoon. Sweat. Bob didn't give a damn. He went swimming and drinking when I got sick. He met other couples. He knew it was over before we got married. He just fucking well wanted to go to Mexico."

What ensued was a silence that stank. The air conditioner turned itself on. I held my breath. I was crying, but I couldn't let them hear me. I sank to the floor behind the dining room table. My grandmother spoke.

"I don't know where you learned language like that. I didn't teach it to you," Georgia commented, without emotion.

Under the table I could see my mother's feet turn around and face my grandmother.

"Is that all you have to say?" my mother needled. I couldn't control my sobs. I knew I couldn't be heard. I couldn't see anything. I closed my eyes to see the spots. There was only black.

"No. I have more. It's simple as this. Your father is in the hospital in New York. With a stroke. You haven't shown any concern for him. You know he loves you. Henry Adams will be proud to see L.P. in military school. He went to one, all our family graduated with honors. Quite frankly, Violet, I don't care about white trash. You have become white trash. It's sad. But you'll do as I say," Georgia said.

Suddenly I felt Betty's arms pushing me up. I was crying so hard I felt my feet wiggle. Betty's arms tightened around me. I couldn't look at my mother and grandmother. I focused on the floor. I saw the wet spot where my face had been.

I felt the two women turn around. There were no gasps. Only a distinct, hollow rush of light and air.

"How long has he been here?" my grandmother asked. It was the voice of a queen. Absolute authority. Life. Executions.

"Long enough," Betty said flatly.

My mother began to heave, almost vomiting. She put her hands to her mouth, not running to the bathroom. She clutched her stomach. I could hear her regulating her breath. Her nose was running.

"God strike you both dead for this." Betty's voice was terrifying. My mother sat down on the piano stool, bending herself over, murmuring "Oh God, oh God." Her scarf had come undone and her black-brown hair rolled out and touched the floor under her.

My grandmother stood up and straightened her back, staring at me.

"Do you believe this, L.P.? You tell me right now you're a big, strong young man."

I couldn't stop crying. My neck was burning.

My grandmother's voice came through again.

"Your mother is a stupid woman, L.P. She's a fool. You say what I just said."

God blinds children when they fall to the bottom of wells, so they do not have to see the mud that buries them. He makes the fall swift and soft, like daylight after a fever, a blindness that cups its hands over still forming mouths, eliminating any possibility of air. They do not have to cry out.

I stuttered and tried to form the words my grand-mother had said. I felt Betty's hands pressing into my arms. The desert revolved below me. Mountains turned indigo, then black. Night birds were waking up, but here they were an echo, a chime of a safer place, with shadows and strings of lights.

"Say it." Georgia stood perfectly still.

"I'm a big, strong young man." My voice was high-pitched. My mother couldn't lift her head.

"That's enough." It was Betty's voice, and I felt her rub her hand on my face.

"L.P.'s coming with me. He loves me," Betty slowly said.

"I beg your pardon?" Georgia asked coolly. Betty walked up to Georgia and crossed her arms.

"What I say now is that child is happy with me. With you both there's unhappy things. He learned how to climb trees. He learned how to bowl. I can take care of him. I'll take him to your fancy school here. I'll cook for him. Just like I do now. I got nobody. I love L.P. like he was my own. Please. I know I can do it." Betty's voice was strong, confident.

"You're fired," Georgia said.

Georgia didn't smile, or betray an emotion. She walked over to her sofa and poured the rest of her Diet Rite Cola, staring at her daughter. Betty stood still, trying to think. Her eyes darted around. She blinked nervously, then looked at the floor. Then she looked at me. She smiled.

I stared at the floor. My grandfather was dying in a hospital in New York, a place I'd never been. My mother was crying and she wouldn't look at me. She wasn't married anymore. The real reason I stayed with Betty was undisclosed. Another secret.

"I want to live with Betty," I said quietly.

"What?" My grandmother turned and bore into me with her eyes. "Explain yourself, young man. L.P.!"

"You don't love me. Betty loves me. You think I am something bad, but I'm not. I try to be good, always. Because I want to be good. Betty knows I'm not bad. She took me to the flower fields. And bowling. And to the movies."

My argument sounded childish and flat. I knew it. I knew something more had to be said.

"I don't love you. I don't know you."

My mother stopped crying and gradually lifted her head. I had to look at her. She pulled her hair away from her face and gradually tied her scarf back, keeping her eyes on me. Her face had lost its color, and suddenly I was glad. I was an enemy now. I belonged.

The living room became enchanted. Four witches. Three hours of daylight left. Dead and dying husbands. Failed marriages. Dark apartments in hot cities. Spells were being dissolved and conjured by eye contact. Speech was not necessary. It was a day for the predatory. A wind had come up and the ninth-floor picture window rattled. Suddenly I was of equal stature. Suddenly they were listening.

If I was a woman, and I still believed I was, then I should come to a parallel. I should have to travel the same roads as Violet and Georgia, only lower then higher. I would get to my destinations faster, but I would see trees, fields of cattle and slaughterhouses in the distance. They would see airports, freeways, state borders. They would never make the wrong turn, be stopped for weather.

Georgia and Violet understood why husbands are left in an August musk, to death and to misunderstanding, to the brown blossoms of summer. They understood why women never stop waiting for rides out, their faces iridescent and random, wasting nothing; walking into a high wind, without coats, through floating newspapers that stick to their legs.

They could check out in a fray of leaves, shimmering

like locust over picked dry fields, and sometimes did. Or stand in high-rise apartments with a view of golf courses and laundromats, waiting for their momentary murders to shift. Such is magic.

I knew that silence was the last time I would be permitted this power. One simple sentence. I did not regret what I had said. I knew my mother had been in town longer than one day. That she had called Betty, telling her she was in town, she wasn't ready for me. It was in her eyes. She was acting a false hurt, a disappearing pink under her lashes telling me this is all drama. I am an actress. Now I remembered how Betty hung up her telephone those flimsy last weeks of August, saturated in heat and purple shade, whenever I came into the room. How she stared at me without nuance, as though she had seen a crushed cat at the side of the road in another city, one she didn't have to be concerned with.

I knew then my grandmother had put my grandfather into the hospital. She had rattled her bracelets, coiled and bit. Then more hospitals, conferences with doctors, explaining what should be done to keep Henry Adams alive. It was something different to do. She could dress up in New York. Of course, there was no time for correspondence.

I glanced at Violet, then past her to Betty, smiling with her. Her eyes had lost their dull haze. She touched my hair. Then I looked at my grandmother. None of the women were seeing one another, but their bodies were sensual and prepared. Like snapping an arm before the needle goes in.

Betty lit a Kool in the middle of the room. My grandmother twisted her gold rope. My mother tried to recapture my attention with her eyes.

"No, L.P. It is not possible." My grandmother's voice. Soft, surprised.

"You heard the child. What does that say?" Betty's voice.

My mother bolted out of her seat, looking like she was ready to slap Betty. She let her arms drop, her face contorted and struggling to seem intelligent. She sat down again.

My grandmother quietly, elegantly, crossed her legs. She seemed quite relaxed, like she was at a cocktail party. She seemed entirely comfortable with everything that was going on, and spoke.

"I said you were fired."

Gray light filtered through the living room. More clouds were coming. I sensed they were an hour away.

At that moment, Betty surprised me. Her body relaxed and she turned and walked out of the room, without a gesture, a secret code to me to keep the magic going.

"It was a bad idea, Violet. You should have told me. I certainly would not have my grandchild stay with the coloreds all summer. You see how she turned him against us?" My grandmother had dismissed everything. The magic was vanished. I was him again. I was in the same room and I became angry.

"My name is L.P. None of you love me," I said.

"Of course it is, dear." My grandmother looked up at me from her velvet sofa. Her eyes admired me.

"You've grown an inch, but your hair. You look like a hippie."

I heard the kitchen door quietly close. Betty was gone.

I knew I should run, but if I did, there would be no forgiveness. I wanted to shatter glass, throw myself into the air. Run and jump off the balcony in front of them. But if I did, they wouldn't care. I imagined Violet reaching into her purse and redoing her lipstick, saying, "Well, that's over." And my grandmother walking into the kitchen for another Diet Rite Cola.

I stared at Violet and Georgia, then out the window. I suddenly realized the three of us were staring out that ninth-floor picture window, because words weren't coming. The storm was too fast to stay, making noise as it passed. I saw starched, livid sheets, billowing on lines in checkerboard backyards, dotting the city like doves unable to fly.

Our faces remained unbetrayed and smooth. This was the continuum, an exquisite, vague malice walking, sitting with us, trapped in our air.

This was the end of the magic act. The last bit of dazzle and chipped mirror before we took our bows. I saw only beacons, not clues. I understood why stamped passports are saved, even when they expire.

I imagined the landscape of South Phoenix scratching itself, as though dying from a rash, then turning to dust, like the abandoned, parking lot coals the Navajo women cooked on. Betty was on a train, watching dust storms obliterate mountains. She had my map, opened to a corner, and she was tapping it with her finger, saying, "This is the way out, L.P. You were right. This is the exit."

I couldn't cry. In that brief vision Betty was humming a song. I couldn't see her face, only her dark hands smoothing out my map. I could see the scars on her wrists, the lines of her palm becoming the crayon roads of my map. She rolled it up. I heard her stop humming and actually sing. I knew I would never see her again.

My grandmother's voice broke the spell.

"Sit down, L.P. Over there." Georgia pointed to an embroidered French chair. As I sat down I felt the dried tears and sweat on my face, making my cheeks mummified and taut. I ascertained then this is what happens when things change. Your face becomes hollow and you do as you're told.

"You didn't really mean what you said, L.P.? You know I love you very much," Violet said, facing me. She managed a smile.

"Of course she does, L.P. She's your mother." My grandmother cut through my mother's little speech and continued.

"Tomorrow is going to be very exciting. You're going to be a soldier, aren't you? You fly out with me and then you get to fly by yourself, just like an adult. I get off in New York to see your grandfather." Her voice was careful and precise. "Then you fly all the way to Vermont. Your new school will be the Vermont Naval Academy. You'll be with other boys who come from fine families." Georgia accented the "fine."

"I don't want to go," I said. "They'll hate me," I said. Violet stole a glance at her mother, as if to say, "See?"

"It's best. Go downstairs. Your mother will fix you dinner, somehow. I'll see you in the morning, L.P. I've got business."

I rose and left, not looking at Georgia or Violet. They had become people to visit. I was already far away, my heart beating rapidly. I was holding a sweet, deep terror that would never leave me during the rest of my life. That somehow, I had almost made my magic work, and it would never reappear.

twenty

I CLIMBED UP to the roof garden on the inside fire escape stairs, which were dark corrugated steel and exposed brick. Tiny barred windows punctured the walls at each floor. I kept climbing, listening to the echo of my footsteps. I imagined these stairs were conduits to a prison laboratory, someplace you never came back from. My skin would be turned into lamp shades, my long hair used to make fake mustaches and beards for actors, or bracelets, or wigs for rich women dying of cancer.

I came to the heavy steel door labeled ROOF GARDEN. I pushed it open, almost panting. Towards the east, leaving without rain, were gray-green clouds trailing their tails to New Mexico, like smoke in a movie run backwards. In the west the sun was certain, not ready to set for hours.

Below me, Phoenix sizzled. Cars sparkled like beetles with iridescent wings. I couldn't see people. I was too high, and it was too hot for anyone to walk on Central Avenue.

I hadn't had my hair cut all summer and it was long and curly, blowing across my face. For a few, long minutes, I sat in a wrought-iron chaise lounge, letting the heat blow over me. Then I climbed over the railing and sat, dangling my feet over the ledge. Below me was a thirteen-story drop.

Carefully I leaned forward to see how far I could go without falling over. I estimated I wouldn't be killed if I fell because it was soft, wet grass at the bottom. I closed my eyes and continued to lean over, letting wind brush my eyelashes, sounds of muted traffic and palm fronds tingling below me.

I tried to smell the flower field of South Phoenix, thinking that scent rises and perhaps a trail of it would hit me and cleanse me once more. I opened my eyes and looked out into the haze and saw nothing. If only I could fly.

I knew my dragonfly wings only came in one dream, a dream of fever, and that those wings wouldn't come again, unless I was sick and ready to die. I sat motionless, leaning my body over, to see if they would sprout again from my back. I pushed hard. Nothing.

I would be on a plane the next day, as if my summer had never happened. I imagined my mother seeing Georgia and me off. She would be dressed in something sunny, with gold sandals and large Jackie O. sunglasses. When it came time for us to board, she would kiss

Georgia and whisper something with a nod of her head and a pinched smile. Then shake my hand.

"You're already grown up," she would say to me, then turn her back and walk toward the exit. She would appear solitary and confused, like any child who doesn't know their way home, taking sidewalks with a deliberate vengeance and a hopscotch precision, checking signs to make sure they are going the right way.

Violet knew the signs. They read "No Way Out" and "Not a Through Street." In Phoenix streets were named after Catholic saints, Indian gods and Mexican flowers and lakes. Violet would turn the wrong way at the airport exit, then walk by again, searching. Then she would be gone, getting into my grandmother's baby blue Cadillac, covered up by a crowd.

I edged closer to the jumping-off point and realized if I wiggled any further I would be gone, in the air like a rain cloud, like a young bird or a ladybug, carried by wind. I swung my legs a little, to feel the air.

I imagined how on the plane Georgia would let me sleep under her sable coat, that we would play cards together and laugh, how she would treat me very adult, carrying on about how handsome I was going to be, how I would break many women's hearts. I imagined the plane would have a rough landing, as she was doing her makeup in a pearl compact. Then Georgia would stand up, and begin the crawl with her alligator bags to the front of the plane. No kisses. She would lean over to me and whisper in my ear, "Pay no attention to me, L.P., I'm only a woman." And the back of her head.

The way her straw hat was tilted a particular angle, like a man's fedora. And she wouldn't look back.

One of my sandals came loose and fell, twirling very quickly down thirteen stories to the wet grass below. I kicked the other one off, and watched it fall, and I noticed they both landed parallel to each other, very close, like shoes put out to be worn. I thought perhaps if I fell the right way, maybe I could land in them, like the movies, and walk away forever.

I remembered my dream of the old roller coaster on Pacific Beach, of kissing a sailor and seeing blood on my mother's teeth and no tracks going down. The air will hold you up, L.P. It's hitting ground that's a problem.

I suddenly understood I would have to walk by myself, with no hand to hold on to. No one would be there to tell me how I should behave. I was a secret girl. I would always be a secret girl, and I didn't mind at all. I looked into the vacancy below me, breathed in the heat, and said aloud, "This is who I am. I'm L.P. Fowler, and I'm going places."

The Phoenix wind echoed and hissed around me, a medicinal air that came from iron lungs and oxygen tanks. I turned to see a large scorpion walking sideways toward me, about ten feet away. It fell down, grabbing the rough cement of the ledge, bracing itself against the wind. It couldn't see. It was hoping to find some sand, a rock, and a fly. I wasn't frightened, as large scorpions were common. I found them in sand ashtrays and in pots of cactus. They were clumsy and slow, and their sting, while painful, wasn't like the small yellow scorpions. Small scorpions were deadly, but large ones just looked at me like crabs with a stinger.

The scorpion walked backwards, almost frightened, and then the wind flipped it over on its back. It couldn't right itself. Gusts of hot air moved it around the ledge as though it were a sheet of paper. I knew in an hour, or sooner, the scorpion would be dead. Then the wind blew the scorpion off the ledge and into the sky. I wondered if under its hard armor there were wings or landing equipment. If it would land in a tree, a woman's hair, the backseat of a convertible or in a pool.

Suddenly I wanted to be like Aisha. I wanted to move to New Orleans and conjure. Watch the stars. Discover the properties of heat, fevers, air, light, dusk, and the deep blue before dawn.

I would chant and pray for Samuel and Betty and Grover and Marcelline and Frank up in heaven. I would remember how Betty embraced me with her long, fluttering arms in her garden, how she told me I was special. I would make medicines from cruelty and loneliness.

Every night, for the rest of my life, I would listen for the night birds, stay awake when they sang, and sleep when they didn't. I would touch everything with dark hands, and learn how to love, expecting nothing in return.

It was Betty's magic, but now, I knew, that magic was mine.